I0535811

Follow Your Neighbor

ᴀ Ɖarla King Novel

By Rosalee Richland

Writing, Editing, and Consulting

Published by Wordsmiths4u

ISBN 978-0-9850129-6-0
Copyright© 2014 by Wordsmiths4u

Join the blog conversation at:
http://rosaleerichland.blogspot.com/
Find Rosalee Richland on Facebook.com

Dedication
This book is dedicated to devoted Darla King readers everywhere. Darla's travels began close to home but she has now traveled many miles. Let's dance!

Acknowledgments
Thanks to so many people who have encouraged the writing, completion, and publication of this book and other books in the Darla King series. Special thanks to square dancers everywhere, and to folks in the Sam Houston Square and Round Dance Association, Circle Squares Dance Club, and Brazos Writers. And, of course, to family and friends who make it both easier and all worthwhile.

Author Note
While Nashville, Houston, Dallas, and Austin are of course real, you will never find the towns of Clearton, Isquith, Forsby, and others on any map. They originate solely from the imagination of the authors and exist only in the pages of this book. You won't meet the characters in the book anywhere, but you might want to meet real-life square dancers if you haven't yet. They are a warm and welcoming bunch.

Books in the Darla King Mystery Series
Hopefully, you will enjoy this adventure of Darla and her friends. If you missed the first two Darla chronicles, take the time to read them if you want to catch up on past events and see how everyone met.

If you're a square dancer or caller, you'll recognize the title of each Darla King book as a square dance call:
>   *Right and Left Grand*
>   *Load the Boat*
>   *Follow Your Neighbor*

Chapter 1

The gun felt comfortable in my hand as I rocked it back and forth for balance. I aimed it dead on and let three shots fly. Each one hit its target, none more than one inch apart. Not bad. Shots rang out on both sides of me. Even with my ear protectors in place I heard them clearly. I lay the gun down on the counter next to the partition and pressed the button to bring my target up to me. I could see the target results just fine where it was, but rolling it forward was my signal that I wasn't preparing to fire again.

Next to me, Paul stepped back from the counter. He still held his gun pointing it toward the floor. That was his signal, I guessed. He looked over at me and I tapped my ear protectors signaling him that I wanted to talk. He reached over and laid his gun on the counter in his cubical and turned to face me. We both lifted one earmuff so we didn't have to yell.

"All this noise is giving me a headache," I told him. "I'm going to head out front and look around."

We were in the shooting range at the back of a sporting goods store. The shop was in front, and I'd been thinking that if I just had some cute workout clothes I'd be more likely to exercise. Now was my chance. Paul could keep shooting while I went shopping.

He had other ideas.

"Not yet, Darla. I want you to shoot with my gun first. You need to practice with more than one so you can be versatile in an emergency," he said.

"Really, Paul, I'm fine." In my earlier life as a Florida state investigator, I'd had to pass firearm shooting and safety exams regularly. I was armed any time I went into the field and had used a variety of weapons. Now I no longer owned a gun and didn't want to.

Paul was FBI though, so having a gun was second nature to him. It didn't matter that I'd just hit the target as well as him. He was bound and determined that I keep practicing. And he was not prepared to take no for an answer.

"I'll trade you," he said, holding out his gun. I picked mine up and handed it to him. I kept my resentment in check as I held out my hand to take his gun and made sure my ear protectors were firmly in place. I turned to the counter, hung a new target, and rolled it into place.

Paul's gun felt lighter and sleeker than the .38 I'd rented from the store. I rolled it around in my hands a little before aiming. I liked the solid feel of the first one, yet I could see how a Glock 40 would be useful if you carried it frequently.

I aimed and took another three shots. My first one was a clean hit, but the gun had no buck to it so I overcompensated on the last two and they were a little low. I picked a different spot on the target and fired another three. Much better. I rolled the target up to me and waited for Paul to step back. He was still shooting so I had a couple of minutes to cool my heels.

I had driven up to Dallas on Sunday afternoon to visit with him. With our schedules, it was next to impossible to find even three days in a row we could spend together with no demands. We'd almost made it this time. It was now Tuesday, and I had to head home to Isquith this afternoon. So we'd had parts of three days, at least.

"Not bad shooting," I said when he finished and stepped away from the counter.

"You too. Maybe we'll have a one-on-one contest next time," he replied.

"Not me, Paul. I'm just a simple square dance caller now. No guns needed."

"I worry about you, Darla. You know that. I just want you to be safe."

"And I appreciate it. Now let's go get some lunch before I head home," I said. So much for shopping for workout clothes.

We checked out of the range and stopped at a Japanese restaurant in the same shopping center. After a delightfully light seafood lunch, I knew I needed to get home. There were things to take care of before the caller convention on Thursday. I'd be back in Dallas for that, although I didn't know if I'd see Paul then or not.

4

I'm not much on public displays of affection, still I didn't mind a bit when Paul leaned me against my car and kissed me goodbye. He flipped every switch in me, and I felt like a school girl making out in the parking lot.

My car was packed and ready to go. We'd driven separate vehicles to the gun range so I headed home from there, but now I wished I had an excuse to go back to his place. Ah well, I smiled all the way to Isquith.

Chapter 2

The next morning, I decided to do some work in the yard. I love yard work and gardening. It gives me time to think, and the results are worth the sweat.

About mid-morning, I stopped pulling weeds in the side flowerbed of my house and looked up at the two cars pulling into the driveway next door. A realtor showing the house, I thought. Soon after, I was surprised to see a moving van pull up at the curb.

The house had been empty for about six months and I hadn't seen any activity at all. Now someone was moving in? I abandoned my half-weeded flowerbed, stood up and openly watched the proceedings. They were going to be my neighbors, after all.

I hadn't known the previous residents well, which was unusual. I knew most of my neighbors, even if we didn't always socialize together. Take the neighbors on the other side of me, for example, Wayne and Jeanette. We had exchanged house keys so we could look out for the other's house if one of us was out of town. I talked to them whenever we saw each other out in the yard and on occasion we'd get together for coffee or just conversation. I'd met their grown kids and they had met my daughter, Heather, now away at school. Because I traveled a lot, I always kept them informed about when I'd be gone. Although they seldom traveled, I was happy to return the favor when needed.

The family on the other side of me, however, had pretty much kept to themselves. I knew they had faced one of the unfortunate endings of a balloon mortgage in the struggling economy. They'd lived there less than a year. Rumor had it they just up and walked out on a mortgage payment they couldn't afford. I had no idea where they ended up.

After they left, someone had come out and mowed often enough to escape the city's code compliance wrath. There hadn't been a "For Sale" or "Foreclosure" sign posted. Now my curiosity was aroused. Who was moving into the house when there hadn't been any indication that it was on the market? Were they renters or were they buying? When I finished my yard work, I'd have to check the MLS listings and see if the house had been sold.

I watched a man get out of a late-model BMW and a woman unfold from a small hybrid car. Hmm, I must live in a better neighborhood than I thought. They were well-dressed and looked more like they were going to a party than moving. I would have waved if they'd looked my way, but no one did. They went into the house and the moving van folks started unloading. And unloading, and unloading. Quite a houseful and beautiful stuff, too, from what I could see.

Isquith is a cross between country and suburbia. Most of the homes are basic middle class with a few ranches spreading out at the edges. The hybrid would fit in fine; the BMW, however, would stand out. Blue collar or white collar, in Isquith people know their neighbors and the crime rate is low. My small neighborhood of Cedar Creek is a quiet little area with multiple cul-de-sacs and a strong sense of community. I hoped these newcomers, whether renters or buyers, would be good neighbors.

The main business in Isquith is technology with a major company, Technocorp. Technocorp established a manufacturing plant and research center on the southern outskirts of town some twenty years ago. The majority of my neighbors are engineers, programmers, and software developers. Oh, and retirees. The rest are mostly the company employees and townies who make up the infrastructure to support commerce, education, and finance.

Covered in dirt, I wasn't exactly dressed for a neighborly visit. I'd give them a day or two to get settled and then take over a cake or covered dish to welcome them to the neighborhood. That's me – the small town welcome wagon, always interested in what's going on. Community spirit I call it. Others might call it meddlesome. It's served me well in the past, so I can't complain.

I looked at my flowerbed and decided I should work in the yard for a while longer. This spring the weeds had taken over before I realized it. Surprising how thick they can get and how hot a March day in Texas can be. I stepped back and surveyed my handiwork for the afternoon. Not bad. The caladiums added a bright splash of color to the yard, and I loved the fresh look of the bedding. Something about the deep rich brown of garden soil when it's just put out gives me joy. The caladiums were a little wilted from the transition, and the bed might need some cedar mulch later. I was proud, nonetheless.

The day heated up so I decided to move inside and cool off. I had pretty much cleared the backyard beds and now the side bed. The front yard would have to wait until another day. I gathered up all the weeds and bags from the potting soil and bundled them into the large trash can near my garage. I took the empty pots, remaining soil, rake, and spade around back across my patio and set everything in the mini-shed. It didn't have a lock, but all I kept in there was gardening stuff and cushions for the patio chairs.

It had taken me a long time to find a small shed that wasn't an eyesore and wasn't any bigger than I needed. Besides, it had to be acceptable to the housing association. What I'd ended up with wasn't big enough to walk into, but it was big enough to hold what I needed to store in it. Since it was just a temporary closet-type structure, not cemented into the yard, the building committee of the HOA approved.

As I closed the shed and headed back around the side of the house, I couldn't help glancing over at the neighbor's. Someone, possibly the man, looked out a window, toward my house. I smiled and nodded. In response, he disappeared quickly. A little odd, I thought.

When I was an investigator for the Florida State Attorney's Office my curiosity was a real plus. I've found out that even though I left my job as an investigator, I can't lose the investigative part of my personality. My name is Darla King. I live between Austin and Houston, Texas, in a small town called Isquith. When I moved to Texas, I changed careers and became a square dance caller. I've been a square dancer a lot longer than a caller.

A square dance caller is the person who directs the dance and provides the choreography so that all dancers are more or less doing the same thing at the same time. Callers are an unpredictable bunch and no one really knows what to expect of them. Most square dance callers are male, so being a female and a caller is even more unpredictable. I like it that way. Calling and dancing are fun for me, low on excitement but high on positive feelings.

As a square dance caller in Texas, I don't need my curiosity nevertheless it just won't go away. That's not always a good thing. Still, my curiosity has sometimes led to interesting adventures and my friends joke about "Darla's mysteries." Of course, they also somehow end up right smack in the middle of those same mysteries.

Once in the house, I ditched my dirt-covered clothes in the laundry room and enjoyed a long, hot shower. Clean and refreshed, I looked out the front window. The moving van was gone.

On the computer in my study, I pulled up the MLS real estate listings for the area. I looked to see which properties in the immediate neighborhood had been listed or sold lately, and what they sold for. The listings showed one house a few streets over for sale, but not one on this street or in Cedar Creek proper.

That seemed odd, so I went to a foreclosures website to see if perhaps that house was listed there. Still nothing, and thankfully, no other houses in our area appeared to be under foreclosure either. I thought that maybe the same builder had built that house and mine. On the off chance it had been listed on the builder's site, I searched there. I still didn't find anything.

It was possible that they were renting but that was definitely not the norm in this neighborhood. In fact, the HOA frowned on rentals. Even if that were the case, the property would have had to be listed somewhere for them to know it was available.

Curious as ever, I changed my mind about waiting a couple of days to visit my new neighbors. I decided to cut some flowers from my garden, put them in a vase, and introduce myself. Vase of flowers in hand and smile on my face, I walked over and knocked on the door. As the man of the house opened the door, I extended the flowers and said, "Hi! I'm Darla King, and I'm your neighbor. I saw you arrive and wanted to welcome you to the neighborhood."

"Uh, thank you. I'm Jake," he responded. "And this is Allie," he added as the woman joined us. He appeared to be about my age, mid 40s. He was average looking, not likely to stand out in a crowd, but not bad looking. He shifted his weight from one foot to the other and blinked a lot.

"Hi, Allie, I'm Darla. I hope you like flowers," I said, still holding the vase. Allie was a petite blonde dressed stylishly and expensively. She looked as put-together as the cover of a fashion magazine. My hair was still wet from the shower and I'd pulled on whatever comfortable clothes I found quickly. I felt a little dowdy in comparison. She seemed much younger than Jake's apparent 40-something years; her air of control hinted that she might be older than she looked at first glance.

"Oh, they're lovely, thank you," Allie responded. I was relieved when she finally took the vase from me. "We'd invite you in, but as you can imagine, we're still a little disorganized," she added.

"Yes, thank you," he added, looking to Allie.

"Well, I'm sure you're tired and have a lot to do, so I won't keep you. Let me know if there is anything I can do to help." I opted for escape as the only way out of this stilted conversation. Maybe I should have waited after all.

Jake nodded as Allie retreated from the doorway. I took my leave and went home, fairly sure that I would not be socializing much with my new neighbors. There was just something uncomfortable about them. Or maybe my active imagination was seeing something that wasn't there as it often does. They had to be tired from moving, and I shouldn't judge on first impressions. I left the idea alone, since I had other things that needed my attention more.

Like the caller convention in Dallas. Back home, I packed for it with mixed feelings. This would be only my second caller convention with fellow square dance callers and I still felt like a novice. I recalled some tense moments at the last one, particularly between two of the callers. The competition between Rob Stanton and Lance Granger put a damper on what should have been a fun and educational weekend. Hopefully, that would not be the case this time, but some callers do have inflated egos. I would mainly be taking classes this time around, although I was likely to get a chance to call a tip or two.

There was an added tension for me this time in the form of Paul Harbinville. Paul and I had been seeing each other for a few months now, but were taking it slow. He lives in Dallas when he isn't in Virginia or elsewhere on a case. He's a top FBI agent; that's a whole other story. When I'd left Dallas after the shooting range, we hadn't talked about when we'd see each other again.

I'd mentioned to him over the weekend that the convention was in Dallas, but he seemed to change the topic pretty quickly. I wasn't quite sure how to take that or if I'd even see him this weekend. Or whether he wanted to see me. Or whether I wanted to see him. I'm a little conflicted about romance. Just in case, I packed an extra change of clothes. Remembering the kiss in the parking lot, I added my favorite Victoria's Secret undies. One never knows, I thought with a smile.

I finished packing and looked over the convention schedule. It ran from Thursday afternoon through Saturday night. Only callers would be there on Thursday. Dancers were invited this year, so there were open dances scheduled Friday and Saturday nights. The rest of the weekend would be a mixed bag, so I would take it as it came.

The session on choreography looked interesting. I could always use some new moves to try out. There were several possible classes on singing calls and harmonizing. A couple of times recently I had called with others and maybe some work on harmonizing would help. I really should do one of the Dancing by Definition workshops even though they aren't my favorite. Dancing by Definition taught dancers to respond to calls from any position. I found the highly technical and precise movements of that format almost as challenging as the dancers did. With a new set of lessons coming up soon, the teaching session looked promising. Too many choices!

For sure, my Thursday afternoon would be full and likely Friday as well. After that were the calling competitions. Was I ready to compete this year or should I just sit on the sidelines again? Deep in thought, I jumped when the phone in my pocket rang. I checked the screen and saw who it was.

"Hello Carlotta!" I said. Carlotta is my best friend and a square dancer with the Clearton Squares, a dance club I call for. Often we room together or hang out when we go to a dance or convention.

"Hello yourself, Darla! Are you all ready for the caller convention this weekend? I'm so excited and glad they decided to invite dancers this year!" Carlotta said. "I can't wait to dance in a square full of callers and hear all the creative calls coming from the stage!" Cute, petite and perky, she was always full of enthusiasm. At the end of almost every sentence her voice went up a notch.

I chuckled and answered, "Packed and checking on which sessions to go to. Some of us will be working, you know?"

"Yeah, yeah! I know. Poor you! Hey, I was calling to see if you wanted to join us for dinner before the dance on Friday. It'll be me and Nick, Sam and Zoe, and Doug… and Cassie." Her voice didn't go up on the end of that last sentence. I heard her hesitation. Doug's a dancer at Clearton Squares too. He and I had dated seriously for a while. It had been a bit awkward when I started seeing Paul, although Doug and I remained friends. Or at least I thought we did.

He'd dated several women during the time I'd been seeing Paul, most recently Cassie. I'm fine with that. Carlotta's always worried I'll be upset seeing him with a date. I put a lot of enthusiasm in my voice to reassure her.

"That sounds great! I'm heading over tomorrow and I'll have sessions all Thursday afternoon and during the day Friday. I will be up for a change of pace and some friendly conversation by Friday evening, I'm sure!"

"Any chance your Harbinville Hunk will make an appearance? Or do we have to have one of 'Darla's mysteries' before we get honored by his presence?" she teased.

"I don't know, Carlotta." I heard the wistfulness in my own voice as I added, "I don't know his schedule or if he's on a case this week or what. He knows I'll be there though."

"Well, don't you worry, girl, the Clearton gang will keep you company if he's not around. Anyway, plan on meeting up with us at 5 on Friday, okay?"

"Thanks! I'll see you then, maybe before. Drive safe."

I disconnected and headed to bed. I'd have to get up early to head out the next day.

Chapter 3

It was about a two-hour drive from Isquith to the Dallas-Fort Worth metroplex and the hotel where the convention would be held. Thursday morning traffic was light and I took my time, enjoying the Texas scenery along the way. Every season has its good side, and the unusually warm spring weather was bringing out all the plants. I passed pastures with brand new lime green grass along with the newly born calves that always make me smile. I saw a few stands of bluebonnets and Indian paintbrush along the countryside. Time went by quickly.

When I arrived a little before noon, I checked in at the hotel and unloaded my stuff in my room. Ever aware of my tendency toward claustrophobia, I had requested a room with a large window. The hotel assured me all their rooms had large windows and I was happy to see the one in my room. The room was small, but the view from the fourth floor gave a feeling of spaciousness. I could see the Fort Worth skyline, which I figured would be beautiful at night. I dropped my luggage and sound system in the room. After a quick comb through my bobbed hair, I made my way over to register at the convention hall.

"Hey there, Darla! Good to see you!" Zach Jameson came from the other side of the hallway and greeted me with a smile and a hug. We met when we called together with Slim Greenville on an eventful New Year's cruise. I hadn't seen him since. Like me, Zach had only been calling for a short time. Unlike me, he was much younger. I thought again how good-looking Zach was. He had on a long-sleeved shirt that covered the tattoo on his arm that I found so distracting.

"Hey yourself, Zach! Good to see you too. Maybe we can do a couple of duets again!" I answered, glad to start the convention with a friendly and familiar face.

"Slim's here too. I saw him earlier and finally got to meet his brother Tom. Speaking of whom …" Zach nodded to the hall on my right.

Sure enough, Slim and Tom Greenville were heading in our direction. Tom's wife, Stacy, was with them. I knew both the brothers, and Stacy too. Tom and Slim were old hats at calling and a lot of fun to be around. They'd been harmonizing since childhood and it was a treat to hear them do a singing call together.

We all exchanged greetings and hugs. None of us had eaten yet, so we grabbed a quick lunch together at the hotel restaurant. Stacy headed out to do some shopping while Zach, Tom, Slim, and I headed to the various sessions.

Three sessions later, I'd been harmonized, choreographed, and enlightened about new arrangements with popular and contemporary music. I was always on the lookout for newer music and I'd learned a lot, but I was wiped out. I ducked out to the hotel's pool area for some down time. As a caller, I was constantly "on," with a friendly smile and good word for everyone. Every so often I needed to escape and let my cheek muscles relax.

It was late afternoon, the sun was shining, and kids filled the pool. There was no one I knew, so I could wind down. I found a lounge chair in the shade and made myself comfortable. As I slathered on sun block, I listened to the laughter and appreciated the worry-free fun of the kids in the pool. I recharged as I engaged in one of my favorite activities, people watching and letting my imagination run free.

There was an older couple sitting under the umbrella and having a cocktail. To my mind's eye, they were celebrating their anniversary. Maybe even their 50th. Every once in a while he looked at her, smiled, and lightly tapped her hand. She smiled back. Like me, they were dressed in casual street clothes, not swim suits.

They were a sharp contrast to the middle-aged couple lying on their lounge chairs. She was slim and wore a modest two-piece swimsuit. He was pasty white, and his plaid swim trunks rode low below a pudgy belly overhang. He read the paper and she had her back to him. She was doing something, but I couldn't see what. If not for the two kids running up every few minutes and yelling "Mommy, Daddy," I wouldn't have pegged them as a couple. If I ever overcame my phobia of committing to another marriage, I hoped I would be like the first couple, not the second.

I closed my eyes and went over the convention so far. Today's sessions had gone well. I had one more to go to this evening. At that point, I knew I'd be ready for a good night's sleep. Great, I thought, I'm getting so boring I'm looking forward to sleeping. I checked the time on my phone and realized I'd better get going.

On the way to my room, I snagged a sandwich at the hotel coffee shop. I munched on it in my room while I decided what to wear to my evening session. I settled on jeans and a yoked cowboy shirt in muted blues and greens. It reminded me of the club outfits worn by the Stepping Squares club in Fort Worth.

Stepping Squares was the home club of Carlotta's boyfriend, Nick. We all met Nick when he was the victim of an attack on Doug's ranch. I was surprised and concerned when Carlotta became serious about him so quickly. Turned out he was a good guy, at least so far, and I didn't worry any more. Even though it had been less than a year, the relationship seemed good for them both. I was a little envious. Paul and I had met at the same time as Nick and Carlotta but we were nowhere near as settled. I had such hang ups about getting involved with anyone, much less that quickly. My emotional walls are solid.

It hasn't always been that way, though. I met, married, and invested all my romantic notions in the love of my life, Clint King. He was a fabulous man, and I thought we'd grow old together. Until my life took a horrendous turn a few years ago and derailed me along with any directions I thought my life might be headed. Clint was killed and, at the same time, all hell broke loose in my professional situation.

It was more than I could handle, and I fell apart. My personal and work responsibilities took a tumble, including my abilities to be a parent to my daughter, Heather. I left my job, only somewhat voluntarily.

It was months before I realized that I'd left my teenage daughter to cope with the death of her father on her own. I still carry a load of guilt for how I dealt with Clint's death all the way around. When I finally clawed my way out of the depths, we moved to Texas. I moved to Isquith to be closer to Clint's parents thinking it might be one way I could help Heather. Ironically, not long after Clint's death and my traumatic exit from my job in Florida, his parents retired to Florida. Ah, life!

So now I'm gun-shy when it comes to relationships. I fear putting my emotions at risk again. I also still carry some unreasonable feeling that getting serious about a man will betray my relationship with Clint. Over the last year I've faced a couple of opportunities to re-enter the arena of romance, testing my fears.

Shaking myself out of my funk, I threaded a thin black belt through the jean's belt loops and fastened its silver filigree buckle. I looked in the mirror and I was pretty satisfied with what I saw. I've always been self-conscious about my rounded figure, but I'd lost a few pounds this year. My salt-and-pepper hair was graying fast. Soon, I'd need to decide what to do about that. For now I was happy with my nondescript short bob hairstyle. It wasn't stylish but it was sure easy to take care of.

I put my phone on vibrate, or stun as I like to call it, and slid it into my hip pocket. My room key and a few dollars went into a front pocket. I stuffed everything else of value from my purse into the room's safe and locked it up. I was just about to walk out the door when my phone buzzed at my hip. I struggled to get it out of my pocket before it stopped ringing.

"Hello?"

"Darla, this is Jeanette. Don't worry, everything's okay at your house. But I wanted to let you know what's happening."

"Jeanette? It's good to talk with you. What's going on?" I asked. Somehow whenever someone starts a conversation with "don't worry," my anxiety immediately climbs.

"Um...well, I just thought you'd like to know. Not that you need to come home or anything, at least not that I know of."

"Jeanette, you said nothing's wrong. But you're making me think something is."

"Oh sorry. Okay, here's the deal. The police just left your house. Wayne took the dog out for a walk about lunchtime, and he had to call 911. There was a man on your driveway."

"What do you mean, a man on my driveway? What was he doing?"

"Nothing. I mean, he was dead."

"Wayne found a dead man on my driveway? Who, what, and why, Jeanette?" Anxiety growing, I paced around the hotel room.

"It appears it was some guy who just moved into the house on the other side of you. That's all Wayne and I really know right now. Wayne gave the policeman your phone number, though, so I thought I better tell you before someone called you."

"Absolutely. Thanks. I'm thinking I better come home and make sure everything's okay."

"I don't see any reason to cut your weekend short, Darla. After the police left, Wayne went into your house to make sure everything looked okay. Nothing was disturbed. The man was in the driveway, but apparently didn't try to get into the house."

"Wow. I'll have to think on that one, Jeanette. Maybe I'll wait and see if the police give me a call. I really appreciate you calling me. Keep me posted if you find out anything else. I'll let you know if I decide to come home early. Take care."

"You too, Darla. I'll see you Sunday. Bye."

Well, this was a bolt out of the blue. I weighed the pros and cons of going home or staying at the convention, and didn't see any particular reason to go home. Jeanette and Wayne were wonderful neighbors and good friends. I trusted Wayne to know if anyone had been in my house, and if he said everything was fine, it probably was. I was sure the police would call me sooner or later and they'd let me know if I needed to head back. I decided to stay for now.

I refocused my attention on the convention schedule as best I could. I was having trouble keeping my mind on the night's activities without thinking about Jeanette's call and the couple I met yesterday. My imagination was, of course, running wild. I was curious as heck, but if I was going to stay here I needed my mind on business. My immediate business was my sound system and what to do with it when I left the room.

Tonight, all the callers would be using the same equipment. I wasn't likely to be calling for the sessions this evening. Just in case, I'd already dropped my thumb drive off with the convention organizers, labeled clearly with my name. I hesitated whether to leave my sound system in the room or store it in the hotel's secure storage at the front desk. You worry too much, I told myself, and left it where it was. I did, however, put the Do Not Disturb hangtag on the outside of the door as I walked out. It wouldn't stop anyone who was determined to come in, but it made me feel more secure. Taking one last look around the room, I stepped into the hallway and pulled the door closed.

I headed down to the Live Oak Ballroom for the evening session on styling. I was looking forward to it. Styling is a surprisingly controversial part of square dancing. Some callers, and dancers as well, feel strongly that dance moves should be executed to the letter. Others are freer in their interpretations and add a little flair. For example, you'll see most experienced dancers adding their own style by doing a swing on a Do-Si-Do call or forming a bridge on a Square Thru call. Neither styling is part of the actual movement. A part of the dance community frowns on flourishes like that. I was interested to find out whether the session tonight was run by pro-stylers or anti-stylers.

The elevator opened and I looked in to see if it was empty. I'm not a fan of riding in hotel elevators because of my claustrophobia. I've been even less of a fan ever since one ride last year didn't end so well. I jumped as I felt a hand on my shoulder and Paul chuckled. Surprised to see him, but pleasantly so, I smiled back. The elevator doors closed without me.

"Darla, where are you headed?" he asked. Before I even responded, he kissed me full on and then pulled me over to sit next to him on a sofa near the elevators. "I stuck my head into every one of the conference rooms downstairs looking for you. I think I even interrupted some kind of meeting," he continued, shaking his head.

Paul keeps me off balance emotionally. Sometimes he seems cool and distant, sometimes devil-may-care, sometimes socially uncomfortable, and sometimes take-charge. I never know which Paul I will see... or whether I'll see him at all. Combined with my romantic reluctance, we make an unusual couple.

"I'm going to my final session now. Can I see you after that?" I stuttered. After a short pause, I added wistfully, "I wasn't sure I'd see you this weekend." Darn it, what happened to that strong woman I had become? I was whining all over the place.

Paul grimaced slightly and looked almost uncomfortable as he said, "I wasn't either. You told me you'd be here, but I wasn't sure I wanted to hang around the convention center while you worked."

At my puzzled expression, he continued, "Yes, I know I've hung around your conventions before, but that was work. It didn't matter that I didn't know an Allemande from a Do-Si-Do. I was just the feebee agent asking questions and doing his job." Looking uncharacteristically vulnerable, he added, "And let's be serious, most of your friends aren't exactly going to be thrilled to see me."

I laughed a bit and assured him, "That's how much you know. Carlotta was just asking me yesterday if you'd be here. Paul, square dancers are a friendly bunch. And as long as you're not questioning them, I'm sure they'll relax and accept you for the man, and not the agent." I realized I wasn't too sure of that when it came to Doug, but I hoped I was right.

Paul kissed me on the cheek and smiled. "So where are your partners in crime?" he asked.

So far, my square dance friends had primarily been around Paul when he was working a case, the cases my friends referred to as "Darla's mysteries." We weren't actually partners in crime, but we seemed to find crime more than most folks.

"Today is only for callers," I explained. "The rest of the dancers will get here on Friday and Saturday." I tried out a come-hither look that felt like it fizzled. "So I'm here all alone tonight. Got any ideas?"

He sighed. "Lots of ideas. Unfortunately, their execution will have to wait. I thought maybe I'd catch dinner with you tonight, but after that I have to head out on a case. I should be back late tomorrow."

"How late?" I asked. "Will you be here for dinner about 5? That's when I'm supposed to have dinner with my 'partners in crime' as you call them."

"I'll try, but I can't promise," he answered. "Darla, we knew this relationship would be tough to start with. We talked about it. Between your schedule and mine, I'm happy just to see you when I can."

"I know. I just figured we'd be able to schedule at least a day in advance," I whined again.

"That's why I didn't tell you for sure I'd be here. I couldn't," Paul said. "Really, I'll try my best to be here for dinner Friday night. If not, I'll find you in your hotel room after dinner." With his FBI status, Paul never seemed to have trouble finding out room numbers. I knew he'd find me when he could.

"So how about a dinner date tonight?" he asked, his eyebrows wiggling suggestively.

"Can't. I have a session to go to," I told him with a sigh. As we stood up, he grabbed me around the waist and pulled me to him. I hugged him automatically, but self-consciously checked the hallway for anyone who might see us. Paul wasn't self-conscious, though, and he kissed me thoroughly enough to make me blush and leave me flustered.

"See you tomorrow. That's a promise," he said. The elevator dinged and the doors opened. I stepped slightly away from him as the older couple from the pool came out of the elevator. Paul smiled at my awkwardness. They were the only ones on the elevator and Paul held the doors open until they disappeared around the corner. We stepped into the compartment.

21

He gave me a quick kiss when the doors opened at the lobby level and we stepped out. I caught a very serious look on his face as we parted to go our own ways and wondered what it meant.

As I was about to enter the workshop, my phone rang. I didn't recognize the number but recognized the Isquith area code. When I answered a female voice stated, "This is Officer Johnson. Am I speaking with Ms. Darla King?"

"Yes, this is Darla King. Can I help you?"

"Ms. King, your neighbor gave us your number. Mrs. Jeanette Prentiss. Has she been in touch with you today?'

"Yes, Officer Johnson. Jeanette called me earlier and told me a man was found on my driveway, dead. She said she had given the police my number."

"Ms. King, can you tell me when you left Isquith?"

"It was about 10 o'clock. I checked into the hotel here right around noon time. I was in workshops all afternoon."

"Okay, Ms. King. When will you be returning to Isquith?"

"I am scheduled to be here through Sunday. Do I need to come home sooner?" I was beginning to think Jeanette had underplayed the event and I better get home.

"No, I don't think so. Just contact us as soon as you return. Good evening."

I stared at the phone after she disconnected. Not exactly good phone etiquette. I was a bit concerned by the call but she certainly hadn't sounded like I needed to rush home. I walked into the session, hoping it would take my mind off the dead man in my driveway.

It turned out the styling session was pretty even-handed between anti-styling and pro-styling factions. The former went through the movements that lent themselves to dancer flair but showed how they should be done by-the-book. Pro-styling callers offered demonstrations of how dancers often added styling to certain moves. They also talked about what it meant to callers who have to compensate for styling in their calls. For a new caller like me, it was very helpful. I noticed sour looks on some of the callers' faces, especially those who'd been calling a long time. I guess no profession is without conflicting views.

I'd eaten a sandwich before the session so I passed up all the offers from the other callers to go out for a late dinner. Instead I went back to my hotel room. I'd been right about the skyline view being prettier at night. I sank into a chair with my feet up on another to gaze out the window.

I thought about calling Paul, but didn't want to bother him if he was working. I thought about calling my daughter Heather. I always enjoyed talking to her, but she could tell when I was worried. And I was worried about the dead man on my driveway! I thought about calling Carlotta, or my sister Julia, but finally just decided to go to bed. After a few minutes I settled in for the night. After a little tossing and turning, I slept soundly.

Chapter 4

Whew, Friday had been packed. I'd participated in both the morning and afternoon sessions, hating to pass up any opportunity to improve my craft. All the calling competitions were scheduled for Saturday, so I still had a little while to decide if I wanted to compete or simply watch the others. The afternoon session was winding down and I barely had time to stop at my room and change for the evening. So far, I hadn't gotten another call from the Isquith police or heard anything further about my dead neighbor. I hadn't even had time to check in with Jeanette.

On my way to my room, I went over the evening's plans. In another hour or so, I'd be meeting up with the Clearton gang for dinner before the dance tonight. I'd be calling one tip during the dance. A tip is two dances run together before a short break, and tonight any caller who wanted to call had scheduled a tip. Mine was midway through the evening. Breaks between tips were scheduled for 10 minutes. It meant a quick out and next caller in, with an occasional announcement, so everything needed to run smoothly. I was happy I wasn't in charge because callers, myself excepted of course, can be an unruly bunch.

As on Thursday, sound systems were all set with laptops so each caller could insert a thumb drive without much interruption. I left my sound system in my hotel room. My thumb drive was filled with more selections than I needed. The main hall would be all singing calls, no patter calls. That would limit my selections if other callers liked the same songs I did, so I wanted to be prepared. Remembering the cruise I'd worked over the holidays, I was willing to bet that Zach would do "Calendar Girl" as one of his six songs. It was his favorite.

I slid my room card into the slot and the entry light turned green. Before I could turn the knob, it turned on its own and the door swung in. I barely had time to see Paul before he swept me into his arms. I didn't even have time to think about it, which for me is a very good thing. I responded eagerly to his embrace. For a while there was no talking, then we slowly pulled apart.

"I made it in time," he beamed.

"I see. Early, in fact."

"How early?" he asked. "Do you have some time for me before dinner?"

"You're the tastiest dish on the menu," I flirted. "I'll make time!"

At 5 exactly, I disentangled myself from Paul's kisses.

"What?" he said.

I reminded him that we were meeting the Clearton Gang for dinner, and were already late. If we were any later, we'd have to explain why and I wasn't ready for that. Was he?

"I get it," he agreed.

Despite a few enjoyable distractions from Paul, I got dressed for the evening in record time and was putting on earrings when my phone rang. I answered it without looking at the ID.

"Hello."

"Hey, Darla, it's Carlotta. We're in the lobby. Just checking to make sure you were coming."

"Yup, leaving my room any time now. Oh, reserve a spot for one more," I said.

Carlotta snorted and laughed at the other end. "You bet! So he showed up after all. Sure, we'll make room. Shall I warn the others?"

"Yeah, you better. We'll be right down," I answered, glad that the gang would at least have a few minutes to get used to the idea of Paul joining us.

"Are you sure your friends won't mind me coming?" he asked, clearly feeling awkward. Hard to believe this six foot hunk was afraid of a bunch of square dancers.

"Yes, I'm sure. It might be awkward at first," I acknowledged. "By the time we order though, they probably won't even remember you're there." I hoped I was right. It was more likely they'd give him a hard time for the whole meal, but it would be good-natured in spirit if only he'd take it that way. I wasn't sure he would.

"Okay, I'll give it a try. I'll even stay for the dance. Just remember that I'm still uncomfortable hanging around with no specific mission in mind."

Paul did look surprisingly awkward as we waited for the elevator. You'd have thought he was meeting my parents, not having dinner with people he'd already met. Then again, that was the problem. He hadn't met any of them in a social context, only as a hard-nosed FBI agent. If he was on the job, I have no doubt he wouldn't be awkward at all. We would, of course, but that wouldn't bother him.

As the elevators opened, he put his hand on the small of my back and moved us toward the rear. Even with no one else in the elevator, I felt the walls close in. I took a deep breath and smiled at Paul sheepishly. He knew about my claustrophobia, and pulled me reassuringly close to him, without returning the smile.

When we arrived at the first floor, Carlotta broke away and walked toward us. She greeted Paul first, which I appreciated, in her fast-paced style. "Hi, Paul. Nice to see you again. Under more pleasant circumstances this time, huh? Glad you could come. Got a spot for you with us for dinner." She took a breath and gave him a side hug, a typical square dance gesture, which took him a little off guard.

He recovered quickly and responded, "Good to see you too Carlotta."

The rest of the gang joined us and, after a little fumbling with hugs, discreetly changed to handshakes and nods all around. Paul was introduced to Zoe, Sam's dance partner for the weekend, and to Cassie, Doug's current partner. Zoe and Cassie didn't have any history with Paul, though both may have gotten an earful while waiting for us. The only tension I sensed was between Paul and Doug, and that seemed to dissipate when Doug introduced Cassie.

Cassie and Doug had gotten to be friends because of a camp Doug was helping to establish with equine therapy. He was using part of his ranch and horses for the camp. Cassie had covered many of the town meetings and talked to all the people involved as part of her job as a newscaster for an

Austin television station. Doug had talked her into taking square dance lessons, although they had diplomatically gone to lessons I didn't teach. Since then they had pretty much been a couple as far as dancing goes. How much of a couple otherwise, I hadn't asked.

As usual, Carlotta was buzzing with energy. She kept up a steady stream of chatter as we headed to the parking lot. In contrast, Sam was much quieter with a quick wit and a dry sense of humor. Sam was a good friend. He was a lifelong resident of Isquith, knew everyone and everyone knew him. He was a wiry rancher trying to kick the ranching habit but having trouble selling his herd. When he said something, his few words spoke volumes.

"Zoe and I, we'll be riding along with Doug," Sam said. I got his point. He was leaving room for Paul and me in another car to lessen any possible tension between Doug and Paul. Sam knew a thing or two.

"Where are we eating?" I asked Carlotta.

"At the Cracker Barrel, where else?" she laughed. Cracker Barrel had become a favorite of the Clearton Gang.

We piled into two cars, Paul and I in the car with Carlotta and Nick, and headed down the road. Although early for dinner, with the opening ceremonies for the dance at 6:30 the restaurant was already a crowded place. We'd have to eat fast. As the eight of us entered and were seated, many people waved or smiled. Sam was the social butterfly of the group and, no surprise, most of his hello's were from women. Zoe didn't seem to mind. In his 60s, Sam was a long-time dancer, often a solo dancer, and women needing a partner for a dance would often seek him out. Many times that included Carlotta or me. With Zoe along for the weekend, though, his dance card was full.

Although the table was meant for six, we squeezed in eight with no effort. Thinking like the caller that I was, I realized our party made up a complete square for dancing. We all sat down, ordered waters and sweet teas, read menus, and ordered in record time. Sam made it clear to the waitress, half stern, half flirting, that we were on a tight schedule and she chuckled in response to his tone.

After she left, there was an awkward silence. Sam jumped into it and asked, "So, Paul, what brings you to the metroplex? Our Darla involved in another mystery?"

Paul looked at me and answered, "No mystery. Except, of course, why she wants me around."

A little more serious, he added, "I live right outside Dallas, so I decided to come on over – strictly a social call." He'd started strong, then ended weakly with, "Hope I haven't put a damper on anything."

Sam started to speak, probably a wisecrack, but before he could open his mouth again Carlotta chimed in, "Paul, you're more than welcome to hang out with us. 'Course, we might make you learn to square dance!"

"That's for sure, Paul. I'd look out if I were you. I barely met Doug six months ago, and the next thing I know I'm learning to square dance and here I am," Cassie added.

Everyone nodded and laughed, and Paul looked a bit sheepish. I tried to help him out and piped up, "To Paul's defense, he's a good dancer. Just not a square dancer... yet!"

That was met with more laughter. As our food arrived Nick offered, "Paul, if you live in the area, my club, the Stepping Squares, is about to start lessons. We're right here in Fort Worth."

With Paul now sporting a 'deer in the headlights' expression, Sam laughed and rescued him by asking, "Earth to Darla. You've got a faraway look in those eyes of yours. What's goin' on behind 'em? I'm betting you have a mystery in swing after all, even if you haven't told your man about it."

I saw him wink at Paul, including him in the joke. "Give it up, Darla Darlin'. You can't go solving these things alone you know. You usually manage to drag one of us into it – first Carlotta, then Nick. I'm ready for my turn!"

"I can't slip anything by you, can I, Sam? It's probably nothing. A couple moved into an empty house next door to me, but there was no 'to rent' sign, no sign of foreclosure, and no record of a sale," I explained and shrugged my shoulders.

"Could be a logical explanation, but they're not exactly friendly so I'll probably never know what it is. Anyway, my neighbor Jeanette called and told me the man was dead."

I suddenly realized I didn't know how he died. My imagination had conjured up all sorts of things, or maybe he just had a heart attack. He had certainly seemed like a candidate for one – all stressed out. I shrugged and added, "On my driveway."

"What?" All the voices chimed in at once. I looked over at Paul. He hadn't chimed in to the chorus, and I had trouble reading his look. I addressed him in particular.

"I was going to mention it, Paul, but we haven't had a chance to talk yet." That much was true. We hadn't spent our time together talking. His kisses hadn't left room in my brain for thinking about anything else. "Besides I already talked to the Isquith Police. They're handling it."

"I knew there was something afoot," crowed Sam. "Tell us all about it."

"That's it, Sam. Really, that's all I know," I said.

"Darla, you could be in danger," Paul said. "I'll call and see what I can find out."

"Oh, please don't pull any of your FBI strings, Paul," I responded. "I'll find out what I can when I get back on Sunday and let you know." I looked around the table. "All of you," I added.

Paul shook his head, but not in disagreement. I could tell he would let it go for now. I wasn't so sure about Sam and the others. It took a while to get them to move on to other topics. Conversation continued on and off as we ate. As I had predicted, the focus was no longer on Paul. I glanced at him a few times and smiled. He squeezed my leg under the table and kept talking and smiling. I didn't find it as easy to ignore his flirtations. At the same time, my mind was back on my new 'mystery.' I couldn't stop thinking about it.

Dinner done, we returned to the hotel and headed for the convention center. Paul hesitated as we walked into the bustle that was the main hall. Since he didn't dance, I wouldn't be marching in with the rest of the couples. I took his hand and we climbed up the bleachers and sat down.

I explained to him about the grand march and how, because this was a caller convention instead of a regular dance crowd, the march would be fairly short. Still, the clubs represented would be obvious by their outfits. I'd had occasion once before to explain to him about the club dress and how each club adopted a pattern for the ladies' dress and the men's shirt or tie, so he was familiar with that part.

I pointed out where Sam, Zoe, Nick, Carlotta, Doug, and Cassie were at various points during the dance, and tried to explain the calls as they were happening. I stayed with Paul until it was time for me to take my turn at calling. After my tip in the main hall, I motioned to him to follow me as I took my turn in the smaller room down the hall. I pointed out Zach when he got set to call, and he did do Calendar Girl as I'd expected.

Paul and I picked up snacks and grabbed some water. I have to admit, Paul was right about being left out. He was sort of like a puppy following me around. Very unlike the take-charge Paul I was used to. I towed my charge back to the main hall to watch the last few tips.

Toward the end of the night, Lance Granger started calling progressive squares. With progressives, dancers move from one square to another until they are in very different places in the hall and often not even with their original partners. I tracked Carlotta and Nick to show Paul what was happening.

At one point, Lance leaned down and handed Slim Greenville the microphone. Lance hopped down to the dance floor and took Slim's place while Slim climbed up on stage. Slim had started out at the far end of the hall with Stacy. I searched and spotted Stacy. Lance would be her partner at the end if Slim managed to get this done. I explained all the goings-on to Paul.

"I'd like to thank my esteemed colleague for leaving me this mess to clean up," laughed Slim as he picked up the pace. Slim began calling, cueing up the singing where Lance left off. Paul kept track of Carlotta and Nick to see if they moved closer to each other, while I did the same with Lance and Stacy. Lance had given Slim one heck of a puzzle to solve. Amazingly, and a credit to Slim's calling, he managed to get most couples back into the same square they started in. Carlotta and Nick joined together at the same time we saw Lance and Stacy meet up. As Slim closed the song, the dancers gave him a cheer. Lance jumped back onto the stage with Slim and they called for a grand circle. I tugged on Paul's hand and dragged him to the floor. We joined the rest in forming a big circle, said thank you, and the dance was over. Carlotta and the gang opted to head out for a late night snack, but I declined. I still had more sessions in the morning. Plus, I had more enjoyable activities than a meal in mind.

I was still rather shy in our relationship. I didn't want to assume Paul was staying over in my hotel room. We were taking our relationship slow and we had a lot of intimate hurdles to cross yet. At this point, sleeping arrangements were awkward. As we got in the elevator, I looked over at him.

"Are you staying tonight?" I asked.

He waited a beat before answering. He turned me to face him and held me out at arms' length. "I thought I was. If you want me to leave…"

I showed him I didn't. When we got to my hotel room, he opened the door with my card and ushered me in.

"You know we still need to talk about this minor issue of a dead guy you didn't mention to me," he said. "But not now." With that, he pulled me into his arms and I couldn't think about anything else for the rest of the night.

I loved spending time with Paul and sharing my world of square dance with him. On the other hand, I missed dancing. Normally, I dance whenever I'm not calling, and tonight I'd sat out all the dances. I was thinking Paul better learn to square dance if this thing between us was going to work out. And I very much wanted it to work out.

Chapter 5

"Good morning!" Paul said as he motioned with the coffees and food to the small table and chairs.

"Good mornin' yourself! Yum, food and caffeine!" I noticed an almost scowl on his face despite his offerings. As I sat down and reached for a muffin, I asked, "Everything okay? You look a little preoccupied."

"So, Darla, tell me a little about these new neighbors of yours."

"What? Why are you bringing them up? Really, Paul, it's nothing. Let it go. I barely met the couple. I'm sure the man was just out for walk or something and ended up on my driveway. I'll have to answer a few questions, that's all. No big deal. Don't get all official over it, okay?"

I was biting into a delicious muffin when there was a pounding at the door. Paul put his newspaper down and got up to get the door. It was almost as if he'd been expecting company. As he opened the door, Carlotta burst in.

"Darla, did you see? On the news? The man who was killed at your house! It made the news all the way up here!" She spit it all out lickety-split and I about choked on the muffin. Paul handed me my coffee and I took a sip. I guessed I knew why he was scowling.

Carlotta sizzled while I stammered, "What...what are you talking about? Paul?"

Paul pointed to the newspaper and for the first time I noticed the picture. It was of my house. Well, really of my driveway and front porch. My mouth dropped and I just looked from Paul to Carlotta and back to Paul. I remembered my mouth was half full and closed it.

"Not at my house, Carlotta. On my driveway. There's a difference. Although I am surprised it was big enough news to make the papers up here," I said. It took a little of the air out of Carlotta that I knew what had happened, but I could tell she was still keyed up. She hopped from one foot to the other, still talking.

"Not just in the paper, Darla. On the TV. That's where I saw it," she said.

"What was your neighbor's name, Darla? The one you met," Paul asked.

"Jake was the guy, Allie was the woman. They didn't tell me their last name. Like I said earlier, they weren't very friendly." I skipped a beat, then asked, "You've already looked into it, haven't you, Paul?"

"That's the name the news said – Jake, Jake Carstairs! Oh, my goodness. Is he somebody important?" Carlotta was still in overdrive, not standing still, and not going anywhere either. She looked from me to Paul and back to me waiting for an answer.

Paul nodded in answer to my accusation and filled in a few more details. Very few, as was his habit. "Yes, his ID said Jake Carstairs. Apparently a hit and run. One of your neighbors called it in. He was out walking his dog."

"Yes, Wayne Prentiss, my neighbor. His wife is the one who called me. He takes his dog for a walk several times a day," I said.

Worried, I quickly asked, "Wayne didn't get hurt, did he? What happened to the woman, Allie? Is she alright?"

Paul waved his hand for me to chill. "Your friend was down in the cul-de-sac when he saw a car going into your driveway. He thought he heard someone yell. Then the car backed out. When he got to your house on his walk, he noticed the man down in your driveway and called it in. He's fine."

I nodded and Carlotta chimed in with, "And Allie?" She was still standing, bouncing in place.

"The police didn't know to check the house next door until I called this morning." I gave him an irritated expression and he continued unapologetically.

"When I saw the paper, I called in to the office. I gave them a little information and they gave me some. The local police now have your house and the house next door staked out in case anyone returns." So much for asking him to stay out of it. I was torn between irritation that he had butted in and my interest in what he had found out.

More knocks on the door interrupted conversation. Carlotta opened the door without hesitation, and Sam stepped in and chuckled in his calm, slow way. He looked around, taking in Paul, Carlotta, and me.

"Darla darlin', what is it about you and mysteries? I'm guessin' that's what this little gathering is about," he said. "Your house is all over the news with not much other information. What's the deal? Have you called Heather yet?"

"Oh, my gosh! I better give her a call quick so she isn't worried. I'll be right back!" I grabbed my phone and ducked into the bathroom. The room was small and I hate small spaces, but it served for a little quiet and privacy. My daughter Heather is a student at the University of Texas at Austin. Her cell phone rang and rang. Eventually, voicemail picked up and I left a message that I didn't want her to worry when she heard about an accident at the house. Everything and everyone was fine. I asked her to call me when she got the message. I looked at the phone and shook my head. What was I thinking? Heather wasn't going to be up this early in the morning.

I walked out of the bathroom to face an even larger crowd. Nick, Doug, Zoe, and Cassie had joined the party. I love my friends, yet sometimes they overwhelm me. And now they were all talking at once and the hotel room was shrinking. In the commotion, I noticed Doug was the only one who gave my bathrobe a second look as he glanced from me to Paul and back.

"Did you reach her?" Carlotta asked.

"No, but I left a message. It's 8 o'clock on a Saturday morning and Heather is not a morning girl."

Everyone laughed, and Sam asked, "So what's next Darla? You can't go off solvin' this on your own you know." At the not-so-pleased expression on Paul's face, he chuckled again. "You do know you're not gonna stop her, right?"

There was ice in Paul's tone as he asked, "Do you have to encourage her?"

Everyone but Paul laughed at that. I couldn't tell how serious he was, but after all it was my house we were talking about, not his.

As if no one else was there, he said to me, "Darla, a Detective Rodriguez at Isquith PD wants you to come in and answer some questions. Also, you need to check out your house because no one seems to know why Carstairs was in your driveway or if he had been in your house."

"My neighbor Wayne already went in. He says the house looks fine, and I think he would know. I guess I need to pack up and head home anyway," I said.

I immediately realized that was the obvious thing to do. Most people would have already done it. I felt a little off kilter and wasn't looking forward to entering the house by myself. As if hearing my thoughts, Paul nodded and said he would follow me home. I had mixed feelings about that, but I'd resolve those later.

Everyone gave me hugs and scattered. It didn't take too long for me to pack everything up. I never did get to finish that muffin. I saw the remains in the trash and must have looked at it longingly because Paul suggested we grab a couple of egg tacos on the way out of town. This mind-reading act of his was disconcerting. After we ate, he said he was going to stop at his place to grab a change of clothes and he'd catch up to me at my house. I generally drive on the slow side so I didn't doubt he'd catch up or even beat me there.

Sure enough, I was just getting close to Isquith when I spotted Paul's car behind me. I passed the Cedar Grove sign and turned in to Cedar Creek. I was about to pull onto my street when I noticed a police car and a KBCX truck. I straightened out and went on down the road before I stopped. At some level I should have known the police and media would be there, but I hadn't consciously thought about it. Paul had told me the police had the houses staked out. That would get the attention of the media. And any media coverage would effectively eliminate the likelihood that someone would try to come back. In a convoluted way, it made me feel better.

Paul pulled up behind me and came over to my door. As I lowered the window, he stuck his head in and gave me a quick kiss and shoulder squeeze. "Just hang here for a minute. I'll go see what I can do."

Fat chance. I watched him walk back and turn onto my street as I got out of the car. With his long legs, he was strides ahead of me but I wasn't letting him handle this. It was my house and I was already beginning to think of it as my mystery. Before I caught up to him, I saw the KBCX truck pulling out and turning in the opposite direction. I finally got close enough to catch Paul on the elbow. He managed to look surprised and annoyed at the same time.

"Okay, Darla, we need to go to your house. Don't worry, the police know who you are." I wasn't sure if that made me feel better or worse. Taking a deep breath, I headed for my house. Paul walked beside me and when we got close an officer got out of the police car and walked toward us.

"Ms. King? I'm Officer Liz Johnson," she introduced herself. "If you would give Agent Harbinville your keys, ma'am, he and I will enter the house first," she explained with a look from me to Paul. Like I wasn't even there.

"I'll go with you," I told the officer. How the heck did she know who Paul was? He and I were going to have to talk about personal boundaries sometime soon.

"It's your house, of course. But I recommend that we go first just in case there's anything that needs to be dealt with," she responded.

I hesitated, then finally handed Paul my keys.

The two of them walked up the sidewalk and I noticed Officer Johnson pulling her gun and holding it by her side. After checking the door, Paul used my keys to open it and they entered. They emerged a few very long minutes later.

"All clear, Ms. King. If you'd do a walk through and let me know if anything looks amiss, I'd appreciate it for the report." Officer Johnson was all business.

Paul and I walked through the house. I didn't really know what to expect, but nothing seemed different or disturbed. I shrugged my shoulders and told Officer Johnson just that. She gave me her card and with a stern glare at Paul said, "As soon as you can manage it, please make your way to the station. I've notified Detective Rodriguez that you will be there shortly." She turned and left.

Paul and I walked back to our cars and moved them to my house, then set about unloading my car. I held my tongue about boundaries for now. I appreciated the help with my sound system and luggage.

"Darla! Oh, Darla!" My neighbor Jeanette was on her way toward me as fast as her slippered feet could make it down the sidewalk. "I didn't think you were coming home early. Has something else happened?"

"Hi, Jeanette. Sorry I forgot to call you when I decided to come home early. No, nothing else. I really appreciate you calling me about the situation. I just figured any reasonable person would come home after something like this, and I like to think of myself as reasonable. Although sometimes I wonder," I answered with a smile.

"Darla, you're one of the most reasonable people I know. The best neighbor! Looks like you're headed into the house. Do you want some help?" she asked.

Jeanette is in her early 70s and in good shape. Still, I didn't feel like asking her to help lug stuff into the house.

"No, we've got it, thanks. Please tell Wayne I hope this wasn't too upsetting for him, and I'll get back to you later with anything I find out."

"Okay, see you later. I've got cookies and tea waiting," she said. She took off toward her house.

When we finished unloading the car, Paul offered to drive me to the station. While I'm a fairly independent woman, not prone to relying on a man, I'm also no dummy. Paul knows how to grease the wheels of the law enforcement machine. So off we went. Paul made small talk all the way, threw about ideas for where to eat and what to do on a Saturday night in Isquith.

I'd never been to the Isquith police station, but we found the building with no problem. Paul didn't hesitate one bit as he parked in an "authorized parking only" spot. I shot him a questioning look and he just commented, "The job does come with some perks, you know."

His hand at the small of my back, we headed inside. I stepped forward to the desk and told the person on duty who I was and who I was supposed to talk to. He nodded and pointed to some seats and turned to speak into his shoulder. Paul and I sat down and I watched the policeman at the desk nod, look at us, and nod again. After a bit he said, "Ms. King, the detective will be with you in a few minutes." He busied himself at the desk with a furtive glance in our direction every so often. Paul squeezed my knee and smiled at me.

A door down the way opened and a man walked in our direction. Paul prompted me to stand, like I needed the prompt, and the detective introduced himself to both of us. He led us into what I assumed was an interview room. Paul began a conversation with the detective as if I wasn't there.

I wasn't happy with his attitude right now. He acted as if this was his "case" when it really didn't have anything to do with him or the FBI. It wasn't his house. It wasn't even his town! I appreciated his efforts to keep me calm, but he needed to figure out how to do it without acting like he was in charge. I'd been in more stressful situations than this one, by a long shot. A few of which he even knew about. So why he seemed to think I couldn't handle it, I didn't know. Despite the fact that it was putting me in a foul mood, this wasn't the time to talk about it. I kept my mouth shut, lips pressed together and not in a smile.

Detective Rodriguez looked to be in his late forties, with some graying at the temples. He went through all the pat introductory comments that I was familiar with from my prior life in the State Attorney's Office in Florida. He obviously had done his homework. He finally got to the point of the interview after thanking me for coming in, at least temporarily ignoring Paul's presence at last.

"So, Ms. King, we do know that you were not home for the last couple of evenings," he said. "Can you tell me everything you know about Jake Carstairs? Any contact you had with him?"

For what felt like the umpteenth time, I related Jake and Allie's arrival at the house next door and my bringing over flowers from the garden. I described the cars they drove, and how they dressed. I didn't have much to tell him. I had seen them for probably less than five minutes. I remembered the name of the moving company on the van. I didn't have much else to add.

The detective looked at Paul, leaned back, and said, "Ms. King, do you really expect me to believe that you paid a visit to new neighbors, brought them flowers, but you don't know anything more about them?"

"Yes, sir. I do. They were not particularly friendly. They didn't invite me in. They said they were busy and I left. As you said, it was a neighborly visit, not an interview," I answered.

He asked me if I could give a better description of Allie. I did the best I could knowing that it wasn't much. I wondered fleetingly why he wanted me to describe her when he had undoubtedly talked to her already. He thanked us both, handed me his card, and we left.

We stopped and got some lunch, did some grocery shopping, and headed back to the house. Later in the afternoon, Heather called and I assured her all was well. Our conversation was short since Heather was on her way to a friend's house and she knew I didn't approve of phone calls when she was driving.

Carlotta called to see if there was anything new to share, and to catch me up on what was happening at the convention. Apparently Sam and Zoe were having a great time as were she and Nick. She joked about all the solo ladies trailing after Zach. She didn't mention Doug and Cassie. I thought that was odd. Then again maybe she was just being sensitive.

We didn't hear any more from the Isquith PD. After a pleasant dinner, Paul and I set about a quiet night at home. We settled down to watch a movie on Netflix. Now was the time, I thought, and muted the television.

"Paul, we need to talk about something," I started out.

"That sounds serious. Did you remember something about the Carstairs?" he said.

"No, but it does have to do with that. I feel like you're taking charge of things and even taking charge of me. That doesn't work for me."

His chin ducked and his eyebrows shot up. "What on earth are you talking about? Do you want me to go home?" he asked.

"Paul, no. Of course not. What I want is for us to talk. You know I want you around. We just have to figure out where the line is between you doing what you know how to do so well and me standing up for myself," I explained.

"I don't see there's a line at all. What's the problem?"

"Well, there's a line for me. For example, this morning when we got back to the house and then at the police department. You just took over and ..." I didn't get to finish my sentence. Someone started pounding on the door screaming "help!"

Paul leaped up and automatically stepped to the side of the doorframe. I was a little unnerved to see he held a gun in his hand. Where the heck had that come from? He signaled for me to ask who was there like I wouldn't have thought to do it on my own.

"Who's there?" I asked.

"It's Allie. Allie Carstairs. Please help me." Her voice conveyed panic.

Paul signaled for me to open the door slowly after he moved to have a clear shot. I thought he was being overly dramatic. No sooner had I opened it than Allie plowed into the foyer.

"I'm sorry. I don't remember your name. You have to help me," she said. She was either scared or she was a good actress.

"Darla," I said. "And this is Paul." Paul had slid against the wall and his gun wasn't visible. I closed the door and pointed into the living room. Allie moved in that direction, I followed, while Paul hung back a bit.

"You said you needed help?" I asked. I motioned to the couch and we both sat. Paul stood.

"Lord, I don't know what to do. I saw ... about Jake in the paper. I was gone." She didn't elaborate on the point. "I came home and I think someone is in the house. I don't know what to do." She wiped streaming tears from her face.

Without missing a beat, Paul pulled out his phone and called Detective Rodriguez. This was just what I was talking about, I thought, irritated and grateful for his take-charge attitude at the same time. While we waited during his conversation, I asked, "Allie, why do you think someone is in your house? And why didn't you just call the ...?"

She shook her head and reached for her purse. With the phone still in his left hand, Paul brought his gun hand to his side with the gun pointed toward the floor. He was obviously on guard. His movement caught Allie's eye and she looked taken aback at the sight of his gun. She stopped moving.

"Okay, come on over," he said into the phone. He tapped the phone's screen and dropped it into his shirt pocket, signaling for her to hand over her purse. She looked at me and I nodded. Heaven knows who she thought he was, but she shrugged. She opened her purse and tossed it to him off-handedly, no longer looking like a damsel in distress. He checked it and returned it to her. She pulled out a compact and fixed her face.

No one said anything. I had no idea what to say with the quick change in her attitude, and I can never read Paul's mind. We heard sirens approaching followed by a single knock on the door before Detective Rodriguez and Officer Johnson entered unannounced. They both focused on Allie, barely sparing a glance toward Paul or me.

"Ms. Carstairs? I'm Detective Rodriguez," he said. He introduced Officer Johnson. Apparently the threesome hadn't met yet, which explained why he had asked me to describe Allie at the station.

"I'm investigating your husband's death." He hesitated, and his next words came out with a formal tone, "I'm sorry for your loss. We need to speak to you privately." He looked over at us. I didn't move, and neither did Paul.

"Someone's in my house," she said. Allie no longer looked afraid or vulnerable. Her attitude had morphed into a slightly belligerent demeanor.

"I don't think so, Ms. Carstairs. We've had a patrol car watching your house and I've checked with the officers.

They've seen no activity. However, I just now asked them to check around the house. As soon as we're finished you can give them the keys and they can check inside as well if you'd like them to."

"There are some questions we need to ask you," said Officer Johnson. "Do you want to talk here, at your house, or down at the station?" She didn't waste time getting to the point, I thought.

"Don't care," Allie answered shortly.

"Fine. May we use your living room?" Rodriguez asked me. He clearly wanted us to leave.

Grudgingly, Paul and I went to the kitchen and waited. More knocking at the door made me peek into the living room, where two more officers joined the party. Reverting to my comfort zone, my brain conjured up a square dance and I realized we'd have enough people to make a square if one more came in. Allie and Rodriguez, Officer Johnson and one of the other officers, Paul and me, and one lone officer looking for a partner. That's where my imagination goes at a time like this, I thought.

As hard as I tried, I couldn't hear the discussion. Detective Rodriguez kept his voice low and the others followed suit, even Allie. After a while, Officer Johnson headed our way. I retreated so she wouldn't know I'd been trying to eavesdrop, bumping into Paul in the process.

"We're leaving now," Officer Johnson told me. With that bare comment, the police and Allie left as a group. No word from anyone else. I went into the living room to lock the front door.

"That was very odd, Paul. Was she really scared or just very good at composing herself when she has to?" I asked. Her quick change in mood bothered me.

"Don't know. And now it is Detective Rodriguez' problem, not ours. I think we can forget about it for tonight," he said. He wrapped his arm around me, kissed me, and did his best to distract me. He succeeded. Our conversation about boundaries would wait.

Chapter 6

Sunday came and Paul left. Each time I went outside, I glanced at the house next door but saw no one. If the police were still watching the house, they must be using unmarked cars. I scanned for any unrecognized vehicles but couldn't find any. I didn't see the hybrid, or Allie either.

I tackled the front yard, scolding the weeds as I yanked them out of the ground. My neighbor Wayne and his dog came by while I was working. We talked about how he saw the car pull in my drive and hit the man.

"What was his name again?" he asked. "My memory's no better than my eyesight. Wish I would have seen more."

"The man's name was Jake. I'd just met him and his wife the one time," I said. I told him I was glad he was far enough away so he hadn't gotten hurt. We chatted a little about the changing times and the weather, too. It was just a quiet day in the Cedar Grove subdivision. Wayne moved on and I finished up one flowerbed. I quit before getting to the others, satisfied the yard was shaping up nicely. I showered and practiced a few new calls, and suddenly the day was gone.

Monday morning I returned to my usual schedule. Every other Monday I call for the Prendle Promenaders in Forsby. Forsby is the other side of Houston, a little over an hour from Isquith. Forsby is a quiet, small town and the Promenaders are a well-established, older club. This was a club night for them, so in preparation I looked back over what I had called the last time. Although some of the members aren't moving as well any more, the rest of them really want to be challenged. It's hard to find that happy medium. I looked over my notes from the sessions on Friday and came up with some ideas.

Since beginning to call dances, I've learned to expect the unexpected. I keep a small overnight bag in the trunk of my car with a change of clothes and enough cosmetics to make it through an overnight stay if needed. I dropped in some clean jeans, a blouse, and fresh undies. Good to go.

After a quick bite to eat, I gassed up the car and headed to Forsby. The drive gave me time to think, and as usual my curiosity kicked into high gear along with the engine. I figured that in order to tell if Allie had been afraid or acting, I had to go back to the beginning. There wasn't a real estate agent around when they moved in. That wasn't unusual in itself, but again there hadn't been a For Sale sign by agent or owner. I didn't know the previous owners well, so I couldn't contact them to see if the house was sold or rented.

A recent news article I'd seen popped into my head. Maybe they were squatters. According to the news article, people were taking advantage of deserted houses and simply moving in. Staying until they were discovered. Sometimes a long enough time of occupation even gave them some legal rights to the house. They certainly were well dressed with very nice cars if they were squatters.

It could be something else, of course. Apparently the police hadn't been able to find out much about the couple, which they would have if a sale had occurred through normal channels. It was possible they had subcontracted directly with the owners and there wouldn't be a record of that.

I thought about all the alternatives and consequences that might come from a sale, rental, or unauthorized occupation. As usual, my curious brain came up with lots of questions. Not that I was going to pursue any of them, of course, I told myself. It's not my business. As much as I protested to friends who said I created "Darla's mysteries," I knew I was guilty of getting involved in things that weren't technically my business.

Fortunately, I arrived at Forsby before I conjured up anything else about my neighbors. Hal and Lenore, long-time officers of the club, greeted me as I arrived.

"Howdy, Darla! It's good to see you. How are you doing tonight? Good drive from Isquith?" asked Hal. Hal's hair was white as snow. He hobbled a bit when he walked, but kept pace with anyone nonetheless.

"I'm doing fine. Not too much traffic this evening and you can't beat this great weather," I responded with a smile as I carted in my equipment. "And how are you doing, Hal? Lenore?" I asked.

"We're doing just fine," Lenore answered. Lenore's strawberry blonde hair appeared a bit darker this week. It changed a little every time I saw her. She still moves pretty well, though her hip seems to bother her some nights. Hal grabbed one of my bags and helped me get set up. Hugs exchanged, they moved to the door to greet members as they came in.

The Promenaders have a tradition of using patriotic music to start their dances, so I found an appropriate song to get started. I checked the time, smiled at some dancers as they gathered nearby and got the dance started with a "Hey there, Promenaders, let's square up!"

There were some folks sitting out, and some playing dominoes in the back of the room. For members who couldn't move as well anymore, coming to the dances was still a highlight of their social calendars. The Promenaders danced in an extension of the local senior center, but not all the dancers were seniors, and not all the seniors were dancers. Several of the dancers waved or shouted to me, and I nodded or waved back while everyone gathered into eight-person squares.

Looking around, I figured it was time. "Bow to your partner, bow to your corner," and I let the music take over. I called them through the melody, while they all sang along. I did back-to-back patriotic songs and called for a break. As usual, I put on a waltz for any who wanted to partner-dance.

"Hey Darla, how's Sam doing? He's one nice looking man!" Flo asked with a wink. In her late 60s or maybe even 70s, Flo was petite and almost fragile looking. She was one of the mainstays of the Promenaders. She was anything but fragile, however. And anything but bashful. Flo had a unique sense of humor, usually spoke her mind, and openly flirted with all the men, though Sam seemed to be her favorite. Sometimes what she came out with was pretty wild.

"Sam's doing great. I'll let him know you were asking about him." I returned with a laugh.

"And how is that Doug Weathers? Are you and he, you know, still dating? I keep telling you, Doug is a fine specimen of a man. He could go a long way to meeting needs, if you know what I mean," she added in a conspiratorial whisper. This was a conversation we had frequently.

I used the same ploy I always did and changed the subject. I gave her a list of options to grab onto. "So how are you doing, Flo? The grandkids? Been doing any traveling lately?"

Flo proceeded to tell me about her grandchildren and great grandchild, as well as the comings and goings of the other Promenaders. She was a sweetheart, even if she did have a few quirks. Finished with her musings, she headed off to talk to someone else. I drank my coffee and looked around. When the waltz started its final verse, I headed back to my gear. Time to call the next tip. "Let's square 'em up!

I called two more tips, each a set of two dances, using a waltz and two-step to break up the rhythm a bit. I threw in one twist to the usual choreography in an otherwise fairly easy routine. Hal commented on it and seemed pleased. I felt good about that. After the last tip, I turned around from my sound system and almost knocked over Flo and Jonnie.

"Hi Darla! Sorry, oh, sorry!" Jonnie often was Flo's dance partner. He was a bit younger, maybe 65, and retired. Jonnie had white hair, a little on the long side, and a wild beard. He had blue eyes and an easy smile, and tonight he sported a Texas A&M baseball cap. He always seemed quiet, or maybe just in comparison to Flo.

"How are you, Jonnie?" I asked.

"Good, good. Didn't mean to knock you over there. Flo, here, she said you lived up in Isquith. Wasn't there a murder there last week?" he asked.

"Someone was killed, but I don't know if you'd call it murder. I guess you could. It was a hit-and-run. How'd you hear about it?" I answered, not quite sure where this was going.

"Oh, you know how news like that travels, Darla. You gonna help the police again?" he asked, eyes bright.

"No, Jonnie. I think I'll just let them do their job," I said, more a promise to myself than an answer to him.

"Aw, shucks. I was hopin' maybe I could be a help," he said. Flo bopped him in the shoulder. We all laughed and I pointed out I had to get packed up. Jonnie and Hal both helped to clean up and get my stuff to the car.

I managed to get on the road with no other mentions of Jake's death and I was oh so thankful for that. I wouldn't be so lucky the next night. Tuesdays I call for the Clearton club and I was sure the gang would ask about the murder. The question was, what would I tell them?

Chapter 7

I slept late, awakened by the phone. I answered, feelings mixed when I realized it was Heather. I was thrilled to talk with her anytime she called, of course. Meanwhile, my foggy brain was trying to figure out whether to tell her everything that was going on, or simply reassure her and ask about her life. I was still trying to figure out how to be a mother to a grown, or almost-grown, daughter.

"Hi, Heather! What's up?" I asked.

"Nothing much down here, mom. Micah asked me about the guy who got killed in our drive. What's the story? Why was he at our house? Who was he?" She rattled off questions quickly.

Holy smokes, how far had news traveled on this thing? I supposed law enforcement released the information in an effort to identify Jake and the media carried it because it was sensational. Now that Allie had returned, I thought the department that released it in the first place might be regretting their hasty action. At least Heather didn't seem too concerned over it.

"He and his wife had just moved into the house next door. You know, the one that's been vacant awhile? I was in Dallas, so I don't know why he was in our driveway. A car hit him, but they haven't found the driver yet. Afraid I don't know much more than what was in the paper or in the news, Heather," I answered.

"Are you sure you don't know anything else?" she asked, justifiably suspicious. I often hesitated to tell her information I judged might alarm her.

"Not right now," I fudged. Really, about Jake that was all I knew.

We chatted a little bit longer. It was good to hear her voice. Although I knew she was an adult, she was still my little girl and I worried about her. Her boyfriend Micah seemed to be good for her, and I asked how he was doing. He was helping her to take college seriously after a first year when she didn't. I wondered if they were getting more involved than I realized. I wondered if I was ready for that. In between my wonderings, we talked about her coming home over the weekend and that cheered me up.

After we hung up, I decided to call Detective Rodriguez and see if there was anything new. I blamed it on Heather's questions and the anticipation of the Clearton gang's questions, but I really was just curious myself. I hadn't heard anything about the death or Allie since Saturday night. I had a right, didn't I, since it happened on my property?

He wasn't in so I left a message. After I got dressed, I went to work on adding some of the choreography from the conference into my selections for the dance tonight. I was playing with on-screen 'dancers' via the Internet to check the calls, when the doorbell rang. I wasn't expecting company, and I certainly wasn't expecting Officer Johnson. Thank heavens I'd decided to get dressed before working. I didn't always.

"Ms. King, how are you doing?" she asked when I opened the door.

"I'm doing okay. Please come in." I motioned her into the living area. We both sat down.

She smiled weakly and said, "Detective Rodriguez asked me to stop by and bring you up to date. He assumed that was what your call was about."

"It was. So what is the status on the case? And on Allie?"

"The case is still open. I assume you know that Mr. Carstairs was shot as well as run over. No motive has been identified as yet, but this is being classified as a murder."

Well, no, I didn't know that. But I didn't let her know I didn't know. Just something else Paul hadn't shared.

She continued, "If not for the house being broken into and ransacked, Carstairs' death would likely be classified as random. Now it appears he might have been a target. Mrs. Carstairs didn't seem to know what they were looking for." She rolled her eyes on the last sentence.

"So ...?" I wasn't sure what the eye roll meant, and I really hoped she would fill the silence. I hadn't known their house was ransacked either. Again I played it smart and didn't let on.

"Personally, Ms. King? I don't believe a word that woman told us. But for now, we have nothing to say otherwise. Her whereabouts that night check out, so she's not a suspect. Far as we can tell, she just up and went back where she came from."

At my puzzled expression, she continued, "We've been keeping an eye on the house and she hasn't returned since she left on Saturday night. We've got her number in case we need to get a hold of her, but I don't see why we would."

"Her whereabouts ...?" I asked.

"We confirmed where she was."

Officer Johnson answered as if I didn't understand what the word 'whereabouts' meant, instead of asking where Allie had been. I didn't know if she really didn't understand what I was asking, or if she just didn't want to give out the information. Or maybe both.

"We'll let you know if we need anything else," she said. She shrugged and I thanked her and let her out. Now I was more confused than before. Shot? House ransacked? What the heck was going on?

I finished my choreography, and as long as I had time I couldn't help going to the usual public databases to see what I could find out about Jake and Allie Carstairs. A Jake Carstairs showed up with an address in Victoria, without much other information. He didn't have a Facebook account and wasn't on LinkedIn. There was nothing that looked like a criminal history in his background. I didn't find any record of that Jake getting married. There was no record of an Allie Carstairs in Victoria, but I realized it was just an assumption that she had lived with him there. Dead end. I longed for access to the more extensive databases I used at my previous job.

I glanced at my watch and realized that I needed to get moving. I changed clothes and ate. I loaded my car and headed for Clearton. I made sure I had plenty of time to stop at the Clearton Café first. I hadn't made it by there in a couple of weeks and Sadie's coffee and a piece of pie before the dance sounded good. Her gossip sounded even better.

Chapter 8

I snagged a parking spot just down the block from the Clearton Café after an uneventful drive. As I entered the café, Sadie smiled and waved me toward an empty table. Sadie had mentioned the owner of the café a time or two, but she was the one constant. She was certainly the hostess, waiter, short order cook, and dishwasher on any given day. Mostly, she was good people with a positive bent on life. I no sooner sat down when she bustled on over with a hot cup of coffee.

"Now Miss Square Dance Caller, how come you been such a stranger? Been weeks since you stopped in to visit!" she exclaimed as she put the coffee down. "So, do you want somethin' to eat or just the coffee? I got brownie pie, apple pie that is to die for, and I think maybe some custard pie left."

"Sadie, it's good to see you too! And you sold me on the apple pie," I answered.

She nodded and quick as a flash, she was back with a Texas-size piece of pie. She checked on the other couple of customers and then stopped by my table.

Swallowing a delicious bit of the pie, I asked, "Anything new and exciting happening here in Clearton these days? What do you know, Sadie?"

"Pretty much the same old, same old. Not much exciting since last fall when y'all got involved with the law. Sam's still trying to get me to come to a square dance, but I hear he's been spending some time with someone pretty steady of late."

I chuckled and she shook her head. Sam and Sadie were about the same age and in most of our conversations she had mentioned Sam a time or two. Maybe it was just because we both knew him, maybe not.

After looking toward the other customers, one of whom smiled and waved in our direction, she continued, "Now that Mr. Weathers, he and his group are starting that camp up. That's pretty exciting. My granddaughter has Down Syndrome and she's gonna be going to the camp for weekends starting next month. They told us they were starting up slow like and wanted to get the kinks out before the summer."

I was glad to hear that Doug's idea for a camp for kids with disabilities and using his horses to help them was on its way. For a while, there had been some dissent in the community with some folks worried that the camp would draw unsavory types. Eventually, the more rational citizens had changed the minds of the naysayers. I remembered hearing Doug and Cassie talking about all the red tape and certifications and inspections and insurance. In fact, the camp was how they met. I kind of missed talking to Doug about this pet project of his, but he shared that with Cassie now. I should at least call and congratulate him.

I must have sighed because Sadie added, "Looks like Mr. Weathers and the lady who's directing the camp are an item. They've come in a few times. Mark my words though, once everything is working smoothly, they're gonna find out they don't have much in common."

I smiled and tried my best to laugh off her comments. I did miss talking and hanging out more with Doug, but our relationship had fizzled. About the same time, my relationship with Paul had sizzled. Sadie didn't know any of that, though.

One of the other customers called for Sadie. She nodded to them, left me my check, and went to take care of them. I finished my pie, not quite as upbeat as I had been when I walked in. I needed to shake myself out of this mood in a hurry. Dish empty, I left the money on the table, with a generous tip, and I was on my way.

When I arrived at Clearton Presbyterian Church, where the Clearton Squares danced on a regular basis, I was still a little early. The door to the fellowship hall was usually unlocked, so I hooked my purse up onto one shoulder and my sound system case on the other and headed up the sidewalk. At the door, I gratefully set down the sound system and tried the knob. It opened easily and I used my hip to prop it open while I reached out for my case.

"Let me get that."

I jumped. I had no idea anyone else was around. You'd think I'd know better than to enter a room without looking. As soon as my blood stopped drumming in my ears, I realized it was Doug offering to help.

"Sorry," he said. "Didn't mean to scare you." He wedged the door open and reached around me for my case. Together, we walked into the room. A table was already set up for my stuff and the dance floor was cleared.

"What are you doing here so early?" I asked him.

"Tonight's my night to set up. We take turns," he explained as if I didn't already know that after calling here for the past couple years. I opened my sound system case and pulled out my laptop.

"You have anything else in the car?" he asked.

"Nope. This is it."

"Remember when callers used to have to lug suitcases full of records and huge speakers to every dance? Times have changed," he said with a head shake.

"Times always change," I replied. I held up my two small speakers and tiny thumb drive as evidence. As I reached down to plug the speakers into the computer, Doug stopped me with his hand over mine. I looked up into his serious face.

"Darla, are you okay?"

"What? Of course I'm okay. What do you mean?"

"Look, we both have had jobs that exposed us to the seamier side of life. I'm concerned about this guy they found in your yard. Sam tells me it's all very mysterious. I'm not sure he's joking, and I'm worried about you if there's any fallout," he said.

"I agree it's a little mysterious. They can't find out much about either one of the couple. Really, Doug, it has nothing to do with me. I appreciate your concern, but I'm fine," I assured him.

After a beat of silence, he said, "Have you asked Paul to see what he can find out?"

Doug's face looked a little like he'd eaten a sour lemon. Mine might have too, when I answered, "No. He's already

53

overstepping his bounds in this situation, so I'm sure not going to ask him to do more!"

At that, his mouth twitched a little. "Okay, okay. I'm just worried about you, Darla. Remember I'm here if you need me."

With that, Doug gave me a square dancer's hug and went across the room to finish setting up chairs. I plugged the thumb drive into the computer and started searching through my song lists to find the ones I'd set up for tonight.

Doug and I had the "let's be friends" talk when I started dating Paul, I was glad that we could stay friends. I valued his friendship, his concern, and his calm strength. I was a bit surprised by his expressions of concern, not to mention his suggestion that I ask Paul for help. I looked over to where he stood at the other end of the room. Tonight he sported a western shirt with a flag print. I had to admit he was a good-looking guy.

"Who's coming tonight, do you know?" I asked across the room.

"Regular crowd, I guess," he replied.

"Cassie coming?"

"She's going to a movie with some friends," he answered with a frown that quickly disappeared.

"You didn't want to go?"

He stopped sliding the chairs into place and straightened up. "You know I'd rather dance any day than sit around in a movie house."

The door opened and Carlotta bounced into the room. Her head swiveled to both ends of the hall as she took in Doug at one end and me at the other.

"Hey, Doug. Hey, Darla." She focused on me. "You know I just love it when you call for us. What do you have planned tonight?"

Her smile was contagious, and the energy in the room immediately ratcheted up a couple of notches. She was dressed in a traditional short skirt as usual, this one hot pink with rows of silver petticoat underneath. Her blouse had a deep V-neck with silver rickrack around the neckline and sleeves. Her short red hair took its own direction, and fit her electric personality. As usual, she could have walked right onto a style show runway.

"You look great! Y'all are in trouble tonight. Remember, I just got back from the caller convention and learned some new songs. I'm going to try them out on you," I teased.

"Cool, I love it! Doug, you need a partner for the first tip?" Carlotta responded.

"Yeah. Know one?" he kidded.

Carlotta rolled her eyes. "I'll take that as a 'yes.' You're on my dance card, cowboy. Nick had to be up in the Dallas area tonight, so I am solo again, at least temporarily."

Although many square dancers come in couples, there are often singles who come to the dances. More often, because of the age of some dancers, one person in the couple might not be up to dancing but both come for the fun of it. In other cases, only one person in a relationship might dance. Others are true 'singles' not in a relationship. In square dancing, we call all those dancers 'solo' rather than 'single' so as not to imply they are available outside the dance. At Clearton Squares, Sam, Doug, Carlotta, and a few other solo dancers often danced with each other or with anyone else who needed a partner.

A crowd of dancers came in as I was finishing my setup for the night. The room continued to fill up, and I went over to greet the dancers. Carlotta was a magnet and people drifted over to talk to her. Glancing at the clock, I saw it was time to get started. I headed to the front of the room to cue up some background music.

"Welcome, everyone. Glad to see such a wonderful crowd. You came to dance, so let's get started. Square 'em up!" I invited.

Three full squares shaped up right away. A fourth square had only three couples and needed a fourth.

"One couple in the back, can we get one couple?" I called out. I was just about to ask if one of the women sitting out would be willing to dance the man's part when the door opened again and Sam stepped in. The room erupted in spontaneous applause. Sam looked confused for a moment, then quickly recovered his trademark wit.

"Well, thankee thankee, folks. What'd I do to get such an enthusiastic welcome?"

"You came in just in time to fill the last square, Sam, that's what," I explained. "Although you might have gotten the same welcome just for being you. We'll never know, will we?" I teased.

Sam bowed to the room, gallantly offered his hand to the nearest woman, and they stepped into place.

Rather than start with my untried offerings, I put on a familiar instrumental loop of music for my first "patter" call. A patter call is one where I call out the moves without trying to fit them into song lyrics. Patter calls give callers a chance to size up the skill level of the dancers so we can make the dance enjoyable for everyone. I knew most of the regulars, so I really didn't need to figure out a level, but a patter also served as a warm up.

Often a "tip," which is two dances in a set, starts out with a patter call and ends with a singing call. After my patter call, I did a singing call to the Gatlin Brothers' "All the Gold in California." It was one of my favorites to call and one that the dancers seemed to like as well.

"Good start, dancers. I'm always happy to be here with the Clearton Squares. Take a break and we'll start up with some new music in about ten," I announced.

I called the next tip using some of the new material I learned at the caller convention, and it went pretty well. On the country side, I tried Luke Bryan's "Play it Again." Still country, yet more mainstream and definitely popular, I threw in Lady Antebellum's "Downtown." I made notes where I needed to change anything to make them smoother next time. For the rest of the dance I reverted to tried and true calls, and the evening went by quickly. I wrapped it up calling to Willie Nelson's song "Stay a Little Longer" and directed all the dancers into a big circle with a Right and Left Grand.

As I was packing away my laptop, Carlotta came over. "Darla, you want to stay at my place tonight so you don't have to drive home?" she invited.

"Thanks, Carlotta, but I'm going to head home tonight. I'm not too tired, and I can easily be home before midnight."

"Okay, but we haven't had a chance for any 'just-us girl talk' lately. I gotta keep up with your exciting life, ya know?" She cocked her head at me and I laughed.

"Oh Carlotta. I'm the one who has to keep up with you! I have no idea where you get all your energy."

"Maybe so, but you're the one with a new boyfriend and a new mystery to boot!" she said.

Sam sauntered over and he echoed the last part. "Darla darlin', what do you know about this man? I know your curiosity so I know you've been working on it!" He chuckled.

"Not much. Neither the man nor his wife seem to have left much of an electronic footprint, at least not with the names they gave. His wife is definitely unnerving, and she's apparently left Isquith. I've no clue why someone killed him or why he was in my driveway."

I shrugged and lifted my hands to emphasize how little I knew. We chatted a bit more, and Carlotta again brought up getting together soon. I gave her a hug. She was right, we did need some time to chat soon. It wouldn't be this weekend though, that was for sure. Heather was coming for a visit, and I hadn't given her much of my time lately either.

During the drive home, I replayed my new choreography in my head. It had worked pretty well, although it would benefit from some tweaks needed here and there. Plus, I just needed to get more familiar with it. Clearton Squares has a lot of good dancers, so I felt comfortable trying out my new calls on them. Some clubs don't do well with change ... just like some people.

Chapter 9

I was almost to Isquith before I changed mental gears and started mulling over the situation with my neighbors. Allie was behaving very oddly, I thought, given that her husband or boyfriend had just been killed. She apparently wasn't there when it happened, and she'd disappeared afterward. As far as I knew, she was AWOL again. Not that she really needed leave to take off to wherever she went or, for that matter, that anybody needed to let me know if she did.

When I turned onto my street it was as quiet as I'd expect it to be in the middle of the night. There were no cars around my house or next door, so I assumed the police had decided to call off their watch. I slowed down to turn into my driveway and noticed a shaft of light between the two houses. It occurred to me that I should call in to let the police know someone was in the house next door. Allie might have returned to the house, but it was odd her hybrid wasn't there. Maybe she'd managed to fit it into the garage.

I pressed the button on the garage door remote and light flooded my driveway. As my eyes adjusted, I swore the light between the houses disappeared. Just to satisfy my curiosity, I put the car in reverse and backed up to get a better view of the space between the houses. No longer a light there. It was now dark. When I looked between the houses, my brain clicked into gear and I visualized the shaft of light that I'd seen. It wasn't coming from next door. The angle was wrong. It had been shining out of my bedroom window.

My adrenaline pumped. I pressed the remote button again to bring down the garage door. I reached for my cell phone and discovered it wasn't in the cup holder where I usually put it when I drive. I'd need to rummage through my purse for it, and I didn't want to park at my house to do it. I continued to reverse down the street for a couple of houses. I slid over to the curb and stopped. I checked that all my doors were locked and reached for my purse on the passenger seat floor.

I finally found the phone, and then had a brain freeze. When I thought the light was coming from next door, I had planned to call the main police line. Now that I thought it was coming from my house, I should call 911 .... shouldn't I? Of course I should. I stared at the phone screen just a second before my brain made my fingers hit the buttons.

"911. What's your emergency?"

"I believe someone's in my house."

"Are you on a cell phone?"

"Yes, I'm sitting in my car outside my house. I'm just arriving home and haven't been inside. I saw a light I believe indicated someone was inside. But it might have been next door instead." It occurred to me to add, "This might be part of an ongoing investigation."

That started a firestorm of questions, starting with my address. I relayed both addresses and was still explaining their significance when I heard sirens barreling my way.

A squad car whizzed past me and jerked to a halt in front of my house and an officer opened the passenger door and crouched behind the car. I flashed my headlights to let him know where I was. He did a quick check over his shoulder at me and said something to the driver. I was still on the line with the 911 operator so I asked if I should open the garage door.

She communicated with the patrolman and indicated I should. Hoping the remote would work that far, I reached up to press the button. I was surprised my hand was trembling. I had to try twice to hit it. Finally I saw the light streak out from underneath the door as it rolled up.

I wondered why the officers in the patrol car didn't move. The neighborhood remained as quiet as before, and when my garage light timed out it was just as dark. I noticed a car coming up the street behind me and for a moment my adrenaline kicked in again. It passed me slowly, parking in front of Jake and Allie's house.

I had no idea how long it had been since I made the 911 call. Somewhere along the line the 911 operator had disconnected. My phone was in my lap and my hands on the wheel as if I was driving. The officer who had remained crouched behind the car the whole time stood up. I took a deep breath, picked up my phone, and dropped it into my purse.

A female figure stepped out of the second car.

Officer Johnson. Although she wore a standard police jacket, the rest of her clothes didn't look police-issue. She had on well-worn jeans and her hair was held up on her head with a clippie. I couldn't tell from where I sat, but I was betting she didn't have any makeup on either. I was pretty sure the 911 operator had roused her from a night's sleep to come out after my comments.

I watched the scenario. The first officer walked back to the second car and spoke with Officer Johnson. I saw him pointing in my direction and then toward my garage. Both of them loosened the snaps on their guns without pulling them out. Officer Johnson started walking my way, and the other officer sat sideways in the seat she had vacated. I couldn't roll down my window without starting the car, so I opened my door slightly as she walked up.

"Ms. King?" she asked.

"Yes. Hello, Officer Johnson. I'm so sorry you had to come out at this time of night," I answered.

"Part of the job, part of the job. I hear ya don't know which house has a prowler, if either one of 'em. What can you tell me?"

I explained what I thought I saw. She asked for the keys and I pulled them out of the ignition. She grunted and turned to walk toward the houses. She turned back long enough to say, "Shut your door. Stay there."

This time I didn't argue. I was quite happy for them to go in without me.

The two officers walked up to my garage, with the drivers staying behind in their respective cars. I saw Officer Johnson hesitate, then motion toward my front door. They turned across the grass. I saw the patrolman pull his gun. She pushed open my front door and they both went in slowly. She hadn't needed my keys after all.

After that, I didn't know what was going on. At first a few flickers of light, what I assumed were the officers' flashlights.

Next my lights blazed on one by one throughout the house. Eventually Officer Johnson stepped to the door and motioned to her driver. He met her on the porch and, after a brief chat, went with her across the yard to the house next door. She knocked loudly enough for me to hear it, waited, and knocked again. She probably rang the doorbell too, but I didn't hear it.

When they got no response, the pair walked around the side of the house. Methodically they shone their flashlights on the ground between the two houses. They disappeared from view and emerged on the side of the house nearest me. She walked toward me while the other officer returned to my house.

"It was your house, Ms. King." My adrenaline ramped up again, just as it was beginning to return to normal. "You'll want to come with us. Here are your keys, but leave your car here."

I tucked the keys back into my purse and slung it over my shoulder. Together we walked down the street to my house. I was shocked to see the condition of my front door. It was hanging open and the wood around the deadbolt was splintered.

"Oh my God," I muttered.

"You want to call somebody before we go in?" she asked.

"That bad?" I asked her.

"Pretty bad. I've seen worse."

"No, let's just go," I said. I wondered if I'd seen worse.

At least there was no body. I'd been reluctant to ask her. In the living room, my CDs were tumbled all over the floor. I'd saved the songs from the CDs I needed for calling to my thumb drive, so it was no big deal other than the mess. All the pictures on the wall were crooked but overall this didn't look so bad, I thought. The TV was still there, and the stereo. In the kitchen, though, the mess got worse.

Frozen food was tossed out onto the floor. All of it from what I could tell, bags and boxes spread out across the tile. Several of my dishes were splintered on the granite counter and the tile floor. The pantry door was ajar and I started to pull it open. Officer Johnson stopped me, and I could almost see her roll her eyes. Of course, I realized they needed to check everything. I peered through the crack. Even though I saw stuff shifted around, nothing appeared missing or on the floor.

"Anything gone here?" she asked.

"Not that I can tell," I said. I bent to pick up a bag of frozen peas from the floor and she pulled at my elbow.

"Whoa, Ms. King. You need to leave that alone," she said.

"But it's melting. It'll make an incredible mess," I said.

"It won't be here long. You have to remember this is a homicide investigation, Ms. King." Her voice was thick with sarcasm. "We'll be taking in evidence for forensic evaluation."

Oh Lord. I really hadn't thought of that. How much of my stuff would they need to take? We walked into the bathroom. It wasn't quite as bad. The cabinets were open and towels were thrown on the floor. Medicines were pushed aside. Obviously a thorough hunt for something. I peered into the office and saw that it looked pretty much like I'd left it. I had my computer in the car, and the rest of the peripherals were in place.

"You think this is related to my neighbor's death. Not a random burglary," I said.

Her answer was matter-of-fact yet noncommittal. "In most home burglaries, the TV and jewelry is first to go. If yours are still here …"

The bedroom wasn't in bad shape either, thank heavens. Maybe I'd stopped whoever it was from finishing the hunt. The pictures were tilted and the bedspread rumpled, otherwise nothing much. It didn't look like he'd made it to the dresser drawers. I checked my jewelry and anything else I thought of as valuable, and confirmed to her that nothing was missing as far as I could tell. It gave me the creeps, but I'd get over it. It looked less and less like a burglary gone awry.

"We've got a team on the way," Officer Johnson explained. "You want to leave us to it?"

"What are my options?" I asked. I really didn't mean to sound flippant, still I think she took it that way.

"You can do whatever you want as long as you don't interfere," she said. "But my recommendation is to go stay with a friend or at a hotel for the night." After a beat, she added, "You can trust us. We're the police."

Still not comfortable with leaving the house, I said, "I don't want to leave the house unlocked all night. What do I do about the front door?"

"Look, Ms. King," her voice softened up a bit. She looked at her watch. "It's almost 1 o'clock now. The team should be getting here soon but they'll be working awhile. If they leave before you get back, I'll leave an officer in the house. Just come back in the morning and decide how you want to take care of things. You can stay if you want, though I don't think you want."

She was right. I didn't want.

"Thank you," I said meekly. "I'll be here early."

I walked to my car, tiredness hitting me in a wave. I was tempted to just sleep in my car, but decided that was a poor choice. I started the engine and drove to the cul-de-sac to turn around. As I headed out to the main road, I passed several vehicles coming in the opposite direction. So much for a quiet night in Cedar Creek.

Chapter 10

I made it to the nearest hotel and pulled out the little overnight bag I keep in the car. When I checked in, I resented having to pay full price for a few hours' sleep but was too tired to negotiate. In spite of my tiredness, I slept fitfully. By 6 o'clock, I was dressed and headed home.

Cedar Creek looked surprisingly normal in the early morning light. Normal workday activity was in motion, and I saw several newspapers lying peacefully in neighborhood driveways. A Wednesday like any other Wednesday for most folks, but not for me. I took a deep breath and pulled into my driveway. A lone remaining patrol car was parked on the street in front. Now what, I thought. Do I just walk into the house?

I wasn't crazy about revisiting the chaos. More than that I didn't want to surprise a cop whose job was to defend the house from intruders. Despite the early hour, I opted to honk my horn for two beats. In a moment, a man appeared at my front door. Still cautious, I waited until he stepped out on the front porch and I could see his uniform before getting out of the car. He was probably in his twenties, although he looked even younger.

I left all my stuff in the car and walked up to shake his hand. After introductions, I said, "Can I clean up now?"

"Yes. They just told me to wait until you got here. Do you need me to do anything before I leave?" he asked.

"Walk with me inside, if you will. How bad is it?"

"I've seen worse," he answered, then looked at me appraisingly. That was the pat answer, I supposed. He was young, and I'm sure to him I looked like an ineffectual middle-aged woman. Little sleep and less makeup didn't help. "But you might not have. I'll be happy to go in with you," he said.

As it turned out, I had seen much worse. Just not in my own house. The place was dirtier than when I'd seen it last night, and about the same as far as what was out of place. I thanked the officer and he took off.

I looked around the living room. Anything with a flat surface was covered with a film of what I took to be fingerprint powder. My picture frames are mostly rough wood texture, so they apparently hadn't bothered with them and the pictures still hung at crazy angles. My CDs, though, looked like a dust storm had come through. Until I sorted through them, I'd have no idea if any were gone. I doubted they would be any help. My mind flashed back to my New Year's cruise, where CDs and DVDs had sidetracked everyone from the main crime. That wouldn't be the case here, I knew.

I was standing in the middle of the room deciding where to start when I heard a knock on the front door or what was left of the front door. My neighbor Wayne's head slowly appeared around the splintered doorframe.

"Darla? Darla, are you here?"

"Yes, Wayne. Good morning. I just got here. Come on in," I said.

He stepped into the doorway but didn't come across the threshold.

"No, I won't come in because I've got Pepe with me. I was just out for his morning walk when I saw a police car leaving. Are you okay?" He nodded at the door and frame. "What the heck happened?"

"I had a break-in while I was in Clearton last night," I told him. "The police naturally think it had something to do with the guy you saw get killed. They're through working here, though, and now I have to start working. Time to get it all back into shape."

He tugged at the hanging wood on the doorframe and it came off in his hand. "Well, now. Sorry to hear that, Darla. I'll finish walking Pepe and be back to fix this. You okay in the meantime?"

"No, Wayne. You don't need to do that. I'm fine, really. I'll get it fixed," I assured him.

"Nonsense. I know how to do it, so there's no need to call anyone. I'll be here in about 30 minutes."

"You sure? Really, you don't need to do that," I protested.

"Too late, I'm coming back whether you want me to or not," he said with a smile. "Want coffee when I do?"

"That would be lovely," I said. Bless my neighbors. I've got some good ones.

I went into my bedroom and changed into work clothes before I even peered into the kitchen. I was afraid of the mess I'd see there and I knew as soon as I saw it I'd want to tackle it. The kitchen turned out not to be as bad as I'd imagined. The floor was streaked with water and mud and the frozen food was gone.

I checked the garbage can and it wasn't there. I opened the freezer. This was bizarre! The ice cream was still in place, sole inhabitant of its cold abode. Apparently the police had taken the stuff on the floor with them for some reason I couldn't fathom. Maybe Officer Johnson just had a little more compassion for me and my cleanup than she let on.

I was deep in the midst of scrubbing every surface within my reach when I heard another knock.

"Darla? Yoo-hoo, Darla?"

"Come on in, Jeanette. Don't mind the mess," I joked.

"Oh, Darla, this is awful. I'm so sorry. I feel so bad that we didn't see anything going on here," she said.

"Absolutely not, Jeanette. I wasn't gone overnight and I didn't ask you to look after things. Don't feel bad at all." I hadn't considered that she and Wayne might feel guilty. "That's why they call them 'cat burglars' you know. They're sneaky. No way you could have known."

She walked over to the kitchen, looking around on her way. "Here's your coffee. Wayne said to tell you he'd be over in a little while. He really can fix that, you know." She pointed to the front door. "He's quite handy. What can I do to help?"

"Nothing really, Jeanette. You don't know how much I appreciate you and Wayne. I feel bad that he's planning to work on the door, though I am very grateful. The rest of this stuff I just need to work through on my own. I know it's silly, but I want to put it back myself just to feel and see it."

"Not silly at all," she said. "I understand. Now you call if I can help in any way." Taking another look around, she asked, "Do you have enough cleaner?"

"I think so. It looks a lot worse than it is, I think."

"Okay. You want to sleep down at our house for a few days?"

"I hadn't thought of that, Jeanette. What a wonderful offer. Let me see how I feel when night comes. I'll let you know."

"All right. I'll send a second cup down with Wayne when he comes."

I was just about finished cleaning up the kitchen when Wayne got there with the welcome second cup of coffee.

"Man, you've done a lot of work already," he said. "I looked at the door on my way in. I can fix the jamb, however the door is a lost cause. What kind you want me to get to replace it?"

"Wayne, I can call someone to replace it. I don't want you to have to go to all that trouble."

"Stop it. I want to fix it for you. Gives me a feeling that I'm being productive in my old age. Tell me what you want or I might get a gaudy one you hate!" he said with a smile.

"Fine. Try to get one as close as possible to the current door as you can. I don't want it to be too noticeable and have everyone who comes in asking what happened. I'll get you the money," I said, and headed toward the bedroom.

"Hang on. I get those fancy reward points on my credit card. Let me pay for it and later on you can pay me back with a check or something. Okay?"

"Yikes, checks. I didn't look to see if he had taken any checkbooks, or gone into my office files. Let me go see before you leave."

He waited while I went into the office. Nothing looked disturbed. The police hadn't even dusted in here as far as I could tell. I'd give it a cleanup eventually, it could wait for now. I made sure my checkbooks were there, and they were all in the order I kept them. I'd call the bank later and ask if there were any steps I needed to take, but I wasn't particularly worried based on what I saw.

Wayne took off and I resumed my work. He returned with some wood and parts to repair the doorjamb. He'd picked up a new door that was so close to the original it wouldn't be noticed. I asked him about the lock. He suggested that he take both my front door lock and back door lock to a locksmith and have them rekeyed. I was grateful he suggested that as I hadn't thought about it. On the other hand, whoever broke in hadn't messed with the locks.

I didn't exactly whistle while we worked, but it was nice having someone in the house working at the same time. I owed Wayne and Jeanette more than a steak dinner. I'd have to come up with something extravagant to thank them. By the end of the day I was satisfied that everything was back in place. It sure was cleaner than it had been in a long time!

With the new locks securely in place, I decided I'd stay at my house tonight. I called Jeanette, then Officer Johnson to let her know I'd be sleeping at home. She said they planned to have a patrol car make several passes through the street for the next couple of nights. Sooner or later I wanted to have a long talk with either her or Detective Rodriguez or both, but it would have to wait until the next day.

I methodically checked all the windows and both doors before getting ready for bed. I was already in bed when I decided that maybe I should leave a light on in the kitchen, as well as outside lights. That would make it easier to spot someone lurking in the yard when the patrol car came by. I went and turned the lights on and returned to bed. I had no sooner dozed off when I thought I heard something. Yup, house noises were louder than usual all of a sudden. I put a chair in front of the bedroom door. It wouldn't stop anyone, but it might slow him down. I managed to get a few hours of fitful sleep.

Chapter 11

Thursday was pretty quiet and, finally, it was Friday. Heather was coming home for the weekend and even though it had been a crazy week, I was looking forward to her visit. I was cooking one of her favorite meals for our dinner that night – steak, a large salad, baked potatoes, and grilled veggies. The vegetables were prepared and marinating. I was cleaning up the kitchen when there was a knock at the door.

I answered the door and immediately was flooded with wildly mixed emotions. Paul was standing there, smile on his face, and that made me all warm inside. But Heather was coming too. I hadn't told her about my relationship with Paul, except in passing. And I had never mentioned that on occasion he might spend the night.

I hadn't even talked to Paul since the other night, so I hadn't had a chance to tell him about the break-in. Judging by his expression, he hadn't found out on his own. All this going through my mind must have taken some time because Paul's smile faded to a questioning frown.

"Uh, Darla, are you going to invite me in or what? I managed to get away and somehow I expected you to be happy to see me," he said. His expression reflected his confusion.

I blushed and laughed to cover my embarrassment. "Paul, I am glad to see you! And of course come in!"

He walked in a little more tentatively than usual. Then he pulled me into his arms and kissed me. As usual, his kisses created a tingle to rival the warmth I felt for him, right down to my toes. "So Darla, I could see the gears turning when you were thinking before. What's up?" he asked.

I sighed and explained, "Heather called last night and she's coming for the weekend. Probably on her way." Looking at my watch, I added, "She should be here within the hour."

"Ahh, so I gather you haven't told her much about me?" he asked with a mischievous glint in his eye.

"Well, yes. Not really," I answered to dodge the question. I blushed again.

"Relax, Darla. Let's play it by ear and see what the day brings. I can always return to Fort Worth tonight instead of staying over if you're more comfortable." He hesitated, scrunched up his face, and asked, "Unless you want me to leave now?"

"No, no. I don't want you to leave now," I said as I moved a little closer and slid my arms around his neck. "I guess I'm just not ready to discuss my 'overnights' with my daughter," I added. I realized that I even had trouble saying that out loud.

Paul laughed and I blushed again, darn it.

"So what's the plan for Heather? Will I be in the way?" he asked.

"Nope. I'm fixing dinner. We're having steaks, so I think you'll like it too. I can put on an extra potato and an extra steak no problem. Heather said she was getting together with some of her friends from high school this weekend. I really don't know what her plans are, but I suspect she'll eat and then disappear."

"How about I take charge of the grill? That way you and she can chat some while I cook," he offered.

I nodded and we headed into the kitchen. He put his arms around me again and I started to melted. I reluctantly pushed him away. I grabbed another potato, washed and wrapped it in foil, and added it to the others already on the grill. That done, I prepared the salad.

We chatted, mostly about the next big square dances and caller labs. Nationals would be in Nashville this year and I needed to book my flight. Paul asked about Carlotta and Nick, and the rest of the Clearton gang. I really wanted to ask him if he knew anything more about Jake or Allie, even though I wasn't sure I wanted to hear how much he had inserted himself into the situation. There was no doubt in my mind that I had to tell him about Tuesday night, but I was putting it off. The car horn let us know Heather had arrived. The break-in story would have to wait.

I headed out to meet her and Paul followed. Outside, I made introductions and we helped Heather with her stuff. She had enough with her for me to become anxious. Heather's first year at UT had not gone well. I thought the second year had gone better. Seeing what she had in her car made me wonder. "Heather, what's up? This is a lot of stuff for a weekend," I said.

"Chill, mom. Nothing's up. Don't worry," she answered with a laugh. "Some of these clothes don't fit me anymore or are out of style. And we got some new stuff for the apartment. I didn't know what you wanted to do with this stuff, so I brought it with me. Plus, I'm bringing home my winter clothes."

Her explanation made me feel better. I stole a glance at Paul and he grinned while he helped unload her car, most of the contents destined for the garage. She directed him which boxes needed to go where. That done, Paul took the steaks and vegetables to the grill. Heather and I sat down in the kitchen so she could tell me her plans for the weekend.

She hedged about why she came up, and told me she was going out with her old friends Brandy and Courtney after dinner. When I asked what they were planning to do, she countered with "Mom, what happened here last weekend? Who was that man? Our house was on the news!"

I wasn't sure if that was her reason for visiting or just a good dodge, but I explained about Jake and Allie moving in, my visit to meet them, and then Jake getting killed in our driveway. I didn't mention the gunshot or the break-in. I told her I didn't know much more than that. She was asking more questions when Paul walked in. I again explained to Heather that I really didn't know who Jake was or why he was in our drive, hoping Paul would get the hint not to say too much.

Paul cleared his throat and once he had our attention, he offered, "Nobody is sure yet who Jake Carstairs really was. But local, state, and federal agencies are working on it. Someone named Jake Carstairs lived in Victoria. That Jake is a retired real estate agent, about 75, and alive and well. The address matches the one on the driver's license of the victim here. His fingerprints weren't in the system so wheels are turning pretty slowly."

So much for hoping he'd stay out of it. And what "federal agencies" was he talking about?

"So far, there's no paper trail on the house or how they gained access. Technocorp owns it, but they deny any knowledge of a transaction, rental, or sale. As for Allie, no hit on her fingerprints either. And no record, other than the statement she signed the night the house was broken into. She split before anyone realized they should ask who they rented the house from."

He knew way too much. Yes, it was a "perk" of his job, and I wouldn't likely get this information from the Isquith police, nonetheless I found it irritating just the same.

As if this was all in a day's work, he squeezed my shoulder before asking, "So ladies, how would you like your steaks cooked?" We gave him our orders and he disappeared again.

Heather turned to me, eyes wide. "Mom, this is scary. Do you need to get better locks or something? I'm worried about you." She leaned toward me and I thought for a moment she was going to hug me. Out of character for her, not for me.

"Now it's my turn to say 'Chill. Don't worry'! I barely said hello to these people so there's no reason to think I'm in danger," I answered with a forced smile. I grabbed my chance for a hug and wrapped her up in my arms. She laughed and squirmed free.

We chatted a bit more while we set the table and got out the salad. Paul brought everything in from the grill and we sat down to eat. I related the little Isquith news there was. I told them about the progress made on Doug's newest venture, the camp for kids with disabilities and equine therapy. Heather mentioned she saw something in the paper about it and remembered the hoopla when it was proposed last fall.

Paul asked her about her classes and UT. Basic small talk over dinner, but I felt a little strained when there was silence. I asked her about Micah and she seemed to hesitate. Then her phone rang and she disappeared. Paul reached over and patted my hand. "She's quite the young woman. You should be proud."

I got all teary eyed as I said, "You're right about that."

He relinquished my hand as Heather popped into the kitchen. Bursting with energy, she told me her plans. "That was Brandy. I'm gonna go over to her house. Courtney's gonna meet us there. I think we'll just hang out and listen to some music and get caught up. Maybe do some shopping. Maybe get some ice cream."

She looked from me to Paul and back to me. "I think I'll spend the night there, mom, so you two are on your own," she added.

I may have blushed as I stumbled on my response. "Tell the girls I send my best, and have fun!"

Paul turned toward the patio, ostensibly looking to see if the grill was doing okay. After a moment, he turned back.

"Nice to meet you, Heather," he said.

"See ya tomorrow, probably around noon." She seemed to place a little more emphasis on 'noon' than was needed.

"Love you," I said with a hug.

"Love you too, mom." She grabbed her purse and took off.

"I definitely like your daughter," Paul commented. He was in a spectacular mood. I couldn't tell him about the break-in now, could I?

Chapter 12

In the morning, we had a big breakfast of eggs, bacon, hash browns, and grits. We were finishing eating and I was trying to figure out how to bring up the break-in, when the doorbell rang. Paul commented, "You don't think Heather would ring the bell, do you?"

I shook my head and went to answer the door. It was Jeannette, laden with a breakfast casserole.

"Darla, how are you doing? I didn't get a chance to check in the past few days. You haven't had any more excitement have you? No more break-ins?" she asked, concern evident in her face. "I brought you over my breakfast casserole."

"Thank you so much, Jeannette. And, no. No more excitement." I wasn't too sure what to do. Invite her in or not. How would I explain Paul? What would she think?

She must have sensed my hesitation and quickly said, "Now, Darla, I have to get back to Wayne. You have a good day, dear."

"Thank you again, Jeanette!" I felt just awful. And she must have seen Paul's car in the drive, though I guess she might have thought it was Heather's.

I returned to the kitchen to find Paul leaned back in his seat, jaw set. I avoided making eye contact with him since I knew he had heard Jeanette and I had to speak up. He was going to be irritated that I hadn't told him about things yet. I put the casserole in the fridge and took my seat at the table.

"That was my neighbor, Jeanette. She brought over a casserole, and obviously we have plenty right here." I rambled with my eyes fixed on my food.

"Darla! What did she mean about 'excitement'? Break-ins? Why was she checking up on you? Why didn't you invite her in?" He hissed these questions at me and I stopped my fork partway to my mouth.

"Well, you know I'm a prude. I didn't invite her in because I didn't know how to explain you being here, okay?

I'm just old fashioned." I sighed and snuck a glance to see if his jaw had relaxed any. It hadn't.

He didn't say a word and I sighed again. "I was just about to tell you about the 'excitement' when she came by. I was a little distracted by other things yesterday and last night. Besides, it's all been taken care of."

"Darla …"

He had relaxed a teensy bit and I spilled the whole story, minus some of the details, like how horrified and terrified I was. I explained how Wayne had fixed the doorjamb and replaced the door. I complained a lot about the fingerprint dust and mess, but assured him that Officer Johnson had been very thorough. I asked him about the one thing that bothered me. Why did they take the frozen food?

"Your house is broken into, ransacked, and you want to know about frozen peas?" he asked with a shake of head. He was more relaxed after that.

"Okay, let's think this through. Was Carstairs ever in your house?"

"No, like I keep telling you and the Isquith police, I only talked to him and Allie once for about five minutes at their house. He was never here and the only time she was here was last weekend and you were here at the time."

"I don't think Allie was ever alone in the living room. Did she use the bathroom or go into any other room? Any chance she hid something here?"

"Not that I remember. We were in here and she was crying. Then she was okay and even a bit haughty and self-righteous. When the police got here, she was resigned. Definitely odd behavior but she only had that designer purse with her and you checked that. We were in the kitchen while they questioned her, but I don't think she went anywhere else." I certainly didn't think she had gone anywhere in the short time she was in the house.

Paul got up and walked into the living area and I followed. He went over to the chair where Allie had been seated. He started to remove the cushions and I commented, "Paul, believe me, short of pulling the stuffing out of the cushions, if she stuck anything in the chair or sofa or on the shelves or just about anywhere in this room? They found it. Believe me."

He shook his head. "Darla, you need to realize that we don't know who Jake Carstairs or Allie Carstairs really are, if they were married, or just two cons. We don't know who killed Jake or why. I don't think you understand just how serious this is."

"Paul, I am an adult and I do understand how serious this is. I know Jake was shot as well as run over. I also know that they've already searched here and found nothing, and I'm fine. Don't treat me like I'm stupid or weak." Now I was the one getting angry.

"Darla, I'm just worried about you. I care about you. You know that. Your performance at the shooting range proves you can handle guns, and I don't understand why you won't get a gun to protect yourself. I have avenues of information that you don't. If you'll just tell me these things, I can find out more about them."

He pulled me into his arms and held me close. It always worked, but it took a little longer this morning. It took him rubbing my back and kissing my neck to turn down my anger. As we started to heat up, I heard a car door close and moved out of his arms as Heather opened the door. Another awkward moment for the day and it wasn't even noon yet.

"Hi mom, Paul. Did you guys eat breakfast yet? I'm starved," she asked.

"Yeah, well sort of. I don't think we finished or cleaned up yet. There's some left over." I added, "Jeanette brought over her super breakfast casserole, too. Feel free to cut yourself a piece and zap it in the microwave. Here, let me help you," I tagged behind her as I moved toward the kitchen.

"Mom, I can get myself some casserole, but I have a couple of questions for you. And you, Paul. I heard some stuff at my friends that you must have forgotten to tell me," she answered with one of those looks that said "gotcha."

In the kitchen, I worked at cleaning up our breakfast dishes and re-telling the break-in story in its simplest form. I left out even more details in telling Heather than I had with Paul. I didn't bother her with the question about the frozen peas. Heather looked from me to Paul and asked, "So are you going to be safe? Is she going to be safe?" Paul raised his hands and shrugged, effectively putting the ball in my court. Maybe he had gotten the message that I wanted to handle this my way. Or maybe he was just afraid to interfere between a mother and her cub. I assured her I would be just fine.

She kept looking back and forth at us and muttered something that sounded like "adults!" under her breath.

"Well, I'm gonna see if there are any summer clothes I left in the closet to take back with me. I may have to do some shopping." With that, she made a quick exit.

Paul and I started discussing the coming week. He was on a case most of this week, and would be in Quantico the following week. For me, that was the weekend of Nationals in Nashville.

We talked a bit about Nashville and some of the fun places to go. Unfortunately, I wasn't going to be seeing the Ryman Theatre or Opryland or the White Horse Saloon. The convention was pretty busy, with barely time to eat. I was scheduled to call at least some part of each day. The only big chunk of time would be Friday during the day. We also discussed whether he might be able to fit it into his schedule.

When Heather came down with clothes in her arms, we had moved on to how we might spend that Friday if he made it to Nashville. Her arms were full and we both moved to help her. Obviously, this trip truly was to exchange her winter clothes for cooler clothes. I suspected my credit card was still going to take a hit.

"I have to run, Mom. I'll message you when I get home."

"I barely got to talk to you, Heather," I answered. Message me, she says. Soon I'd forget what her voice sounded like. "Do you really have to leave now? I thought you would stay the whole weekend."

"I know, but I decided to make it a quick trip. I talked to Micah and he wants to do something tonight. Sorry. I'll call later. Really," she promised.

With her car loaded up, she gave me a hug. She looked at Paul awkwardly and he helped her out by offering his hand. After the exchange of "nice to meet you" and other pleasantries, Heather got in her car and drove away. Paul and I chatted some more and then he was on his way as well. I felt abandoned and relieved at the same time.

Alone in the house again, I washed the dishes and cleaned up, until I just fizzled out. I was completely drained. I was also worried that something else was going on with Heather. It wasn't like her to cut her plans short. I hoped it wasn't because Paul was here.

I looked out at the yard and thought about finishing some of the flower beds, but didn't have the energy. I put on the television and let it make noise in the background while I contemplated all my questions – from Jake's murder to my relationship with Paul, to what I could do for Jeanette and Wayne.

The latter was the easiest once I remembered their favorite restaurant. A gift card would give them the opportunity to go there without waiting for a birthday or special occasion. I'd put it into a bouquet of flowers from my yard and take it over to them. I owed them plenty more. This would do for a start. If only all my questions had such simple answers.

The rest of the weekend was uneventful and I managed to spend some time working on choreography for some of the new songs. I also spent a lot of time on my computer, trying to find more information about Jake and Allie. Not much luck on that. I even checked out security systems, but I really didn't want to admit I was that nervous.

Chapter 13

Monday was a catch-up day. I ran errands, worked on more new choreography, caught up on some reading, and paid bills. Tuesday night in Clearton, Carlotta and I met for a light snack at the Clearton Café before the dance. Our own "girl time." We talked some about the upcoming trip to Nashville, and then she went for the kill.

"So, Darla, what is the story with you and Paul? Is this serious? Come on, tell me all!"

"Now Carlotta, you know I could ask the same about you and Nick?" I teased back, hoping to shift the attention to her love life instead of mine.

"No you don't! Nick and I are old news in comparison. We see each other when his work assignments let us. We both wish we could see each other more often, but we're taking it slow." She sounded content with that and hesitated before sniping, "Now we've got that outta the way, talk."

I let out a deep sigh and put a smile on my face. "Like you and Nick, Paul and I see each other when our work schedules allow. Sometimes he's in Virginia, sometimes in Dallas, and sometimes I don't know where he is. It's complicated." I knew my smile didn't last through that. Apparently she saw it fade.

"So what's the problem Darla? Do you want to see him more or less, or what? I get the feeling there's a big 'but' there somewhere."

"Yeah, well. Like I said, it's complicated. Sometimes I like Paul a lot. Sometimes I just want to kill him!" There, I said it.

At my raised voice, Sadie darted over to our table. "Everything alright here? Your salad okay?" We reassured her and I went back to eating. Carlotta is not one to give up though.

"So what exactly is it that makes you crazy? He leave the seat up on the toilet? Squeeze the toothpaste? Not help around the house? I've dated men like that, they're trainable."

"I wish it were those little things. Carlotta, I'm a grown woman. I've gotten used to doing things on my own, handling my own stuff. He walks in and the next thing I know, he's deciding what I'm doing, how this problem or that one should be handled. Even with Jake Carstairs' death, he got mad when I didn't tell him. He went behind my back and called the police to get information. He doesn't wait to be asked. He just jumps into my business. It's irritating."

Much as I had tried to keep my voice to a whisper, it was obvious from Sadie's expression that I hadn't done a very good job. I smiled at her across the room, shook my head, and took out my wallet. Carlotta didn't have much to say in response to my outcry, but patted my hand uncharacteristically.

As Sadie showed up with our check, Carlotta said, "You know, in his job, he probably needs to be that way. I bet he's just trying to be helpful. Think about it, Darla. I bet you'd be just as pissed if he didn't try to help."

I smiled up at Sadie. "We're talking about men troubles," I explained.

"I could tell," she said. She hesitated and then, as she took our money for the meal, offered, "I don't know what man has you all upset Darla. I sure hope it's not that Mr. Weathers. He's such a sweetheart." She nodded and walked away.

I was dumbfounded and speechless, but not Carlotta. She immediately burst out laughing and seconds later I couldn't help joining in. Obviously, Sadie didn't know the backstory of our almost romance. And of course there was the matter of Cassie.

Shaking my head, I stood up. "Come on, I have a square dance to call and that always makes me feel better!"

The dance did make me feel better. Cassie made it this week and she seemed to be picking up the moves easily. I watched her and Doug dancing a waltz between tips and felt a twinge. It had been a while since Paul and I had gone dancing. Maybe that was part of our problem. We needed more time with just the two of us.

I tried out the new arrangement I had created to Lee Ann Womack's "I Hope You Dance" with only a few problems. My second attempts at "Play it Again" and "Downtown" went much better. I'd be able to try them again in Nashville with a little more confidence. And everyone buzzed about Nationals coming up.

I left Clearton in good spirits, focused on the future. I had forced the break-in last week to the back of my mind, and I didn't mention it to any of the Clearton gang. Nonetheless, it all came back to me as I pulled into my driveway. I broke into a sweat. Everything looked like normal. No lights other than the ones I left on. I pressed the button on the remote and watched the door go up. I got out of my car and walked tentatively around to the front of my house, cell phone in hand. The door looked intact and I breathed a bit easier. I gladly returned to the well-lit garage and went in. Inside all was well. No mess, no uninvited guests. I flopped down into a chair for a few minutes. Before making way to bed and sleep, I sent a good-night text to Paul.

Chapter 14

The rest of the week flew by. I needed to do laundry and pack for Nashville. I thought about shopping for a new outfit or two, but I decided to wait and see what the vendors had at the convention. Officer Johnson stopped by Wednesday afternoon to check on me. She basically told me they had no clue as to who broke into my house or why. She offered to go with me to a practice range if I decided to get a gun. That wasn't surprising given that many people in Texas have guns. I thanked her without bothering to tell her I was experienced with guns.

I let her know I'd be gone over the weekend. Officer Johnson, in turn, said she'd put in a request to keep an eye on the house while I was gone. That made me feel a little better. I sure didn't want to get a call while I was at Nationals. I needed to tell Jeannette and Wayne as well, although I was concerned about asking them to look after things this time. I'd feel responsible if anything happened to them.

I talked to Heather for a bit as well. She asked about Paul and I got flustered. Part of it, I guess, was the mother-daughter thing when talking about romance. But another part of it was a holdover from Clint's death and feeling guilty that I might have someone new in my life. I asked if it bothered her that he had been at the house over the weekend, if that was why she left. She said no. She seemed okay with it, even if I wasn't. She said he seemed nice in a take-charge sort of way. I'm not sure she caught my groan or sarcasm when I agreed with her.

I made sure she knew I'd be away this weekend as well. She didn't come home often, but I told her if she decided to come home while I wasn't here, she'd need to check in with Officer Johnson first, and gave her the number. I'd hate to see the police throttle her if she came while they were watching the house.

I went ahead and called Jeanette and Wayne to let them know my schedule. "Don't come over here if you see something you think is wrong," I warned Jeanette. "Just call the police directly. Lord knows I don't want you or Wayne getting hurt!" I gave her the nonemergency police number, but told her not to hesitate to call 911 if need be.

With the Trail End dance on Thursday before Nationals, my flight was mid-morning out of Dallas with arrival in Nashville just after lunchtime. I had a room at the Nashville Hilton, not too far from the Convention Center. Both were located downtown, which promised the opportunity for a variety of places to eat and hear some good, or not so good, music.

The Clearton gang was meeting me at the airport, Dallas being the most convenient departure spot for all of us. Always a little anxious about traffic, airport security, and hassles with baggage, I was at the airport early. I found my gate and checked the status several times. Finally, I found a seat and decided to review choreography while I waited.

Carlotta and Nick arrived first. Carlotta was excited and immediately started talking about Nashville. Mid-sentence she stopped.

"Wow. Who's that woman? She's dressed in clothes that cost more than I make in a month. From the Valentino suit to the Prada shoes and bag. And she certainly didn't do her own hair. Look at that jewelry! She must be a celebrity, maybe an actress, but I don't recognize her. Who is she? You need to take a look. Darla, don't be too obvious. Do you recognize her?"

I barely followed designer names, jeans being my usual apparel, and I was sorely behind the times on current celebrities. To keep Carlotta happy, I sat up a bit and glanced over my shoulder. My jaw dropped and I turned to Carlotta so fast I almost fell off the chair. The 'celebrity' was none other than Allie. What was she doing here? Could she have seen the information flyer on the convention that night she was at my house?

"Darla, you look like you've seen a ghost. Do you recognize her?" Carlotta asked in a not quite whisper.

"Shhh. Yes, I recognize her, but don't look at her. I'll tell you after she gets on her flight. Be cool."

Nick looked a bit confused. He had heard the urgency in my voice and came through like a trouper. As Carlotta was about to open her mouth again, he pulled her toward him and planted a kiss. She didn't seem to mind. He suggested we all go for a short walk to the expensive airport store and grab some water. In a corner of the store, I told them who the woman was. I also took the opportunity to call Officer Johnson. She wasn't there, so I left a message.

After thinking about it a few minutes, I texted Paul. I know I said I didn't want him involved, but he already was, wasn't he? And he'd said she had disappeared. I let him know she might be getting on the flight at the next gate to New York. That was more likely than Nashville.

The three of us walked back toward the gate and found Doug, Sam, Zoe, and some other dancers. We got caught up in all the greetings and excitement for some time. I looked around once or twice and didn't spot Allie, but I didn't look too hard. Several other flights boarded and took off. I assumed she was on one of them.

Sam had secured an advance copy of the program and we all wanted to know what was happening when. One thing was for sure, if you could dance it, it was happening sometime. There was clogging, line dancing, square dancing, round dancing, and at least one night, a band for just plain dancing! Someone, Zoe I think, asked about the after parties – those are the parties after the main square dances each night. Most weren't listed, since they tend to be informal affairs, but a few were scheduled until after midnight.

Somewhere during our discussions, I heard the boarding announcement for first class passengers, families with children, active military, and anyone else considered VIPs by the airline. I hated to interrupt our little group's enthusiasm, but we were the next block up. Traveling economy wasn't fun for me, especially with airlines now charging extra for seats near the front of the plane. So, claustrophobia and all, I took my seat in the bowels of the plane. At least I had booked an aisle seat. At least it would be a short flight.

We got in line, still talking and laughing, and boarded. If my carry-on hadn't gotten hung up on one of the enviously wide seats I might have missed her, but there in first class, pretty as you please, was Allie. She glanced my way and then concentrated her gaze out the window. I was sure she recognized me but she made a show like she hadn't. This was creepy, her being on my plane. I hadn't put my phone in airplane mode yet, so when I reached my seat I sent another quick text to Paul. I hadn't gotten a reply from my earlier text. Then again, I didn't know if he was checking his phone or not.

I could tell from Carlotta's expression that she had spotted Allie as well. Carlotta passed the word to Nick and Sam that Allie was on the plane. When Doug and Cassie boarded, one of our group must have told them as well, since Doug shot a look my way and nodded his head toward the front of the plane.

Other than the obvious – that she was the wife of my dead neighbor, and my neighbor herself – I wasn't sure why we cared. The main reason, I suppose, was my curiosity. She was supposed to have 'disappeared' and I wanted to know why she was headed to Nashville at the same time as us. It seemed a little coincidental and I thought about the flyer for the convention again. She could have seen it. As a grown woman she certainly had the right to go where she wanted. As far as I knew, she wasn't a suspect. Then again, from what Paul had said, no one really knew who she was and the police didn't even have her fingerprints.

By the time we deplaned in Nashville, we were all on alert to see if we could spot her again and keep track of where she went. Unfortunately, first class passengers get a head start on those of us in economy, and in a city as big and bustling as Nashville we weren't likely to run into her.

As we got in line for shared cabs, Allie was the topic of conversation. Everyone grumbled that she had vanished, and the convention seemed to take a back seat. It didn't take long to get cabs to the hotel. Carlotta suggested dinner at a local restaurant around 6 and everyone else agreed. I opted out. I needed to be at the Convention Center and get my bearings by 6. From the lobby, we all went our separate ways.

My room wasn't too small, but not exactly huge either. I took a deep breath to relax and as I started to unpack I remembered to take my phone off airplane mode. I had a text from Paul that he would be in Nashville as soon as he could. That made me smile, a smile that faded immediately when I questioned if he was coming to see me or because of the case and Allie.

Chapter 15

After a quick nap, I went down to the hotel restaurant for a bite to eat. It was only 5, and with all the other options nearby, I wasn't surprised that it was almost deserted. I asked the hostess for a table with a view. I knew from experience they tended to seat singles in the least desirable locations. We were exchanging pleasantries when I heard someone call my name.

"Darla, right? I thought I saw you on the plane. What a coincidence." Allie's syrupy tone was so fake I felt the hairs on the back of my neck stand up. I was, however, brought up to be polite. And, of course, there was my curiosity to appease.

"Hi, Allie. Yes, I saw you on the plane as well. I wasn't sure you recognized me."

"Now, Darla, you don't want to eat alone. I have a table right over here."

The hostess took her cue and we headed for her table. It was against a wall, in the corner, which I suppose was the reason I hadn't seen her right away.

I smiled at her and sat down. I thanked the hostess for my menu and tried to settle my nerves. "So, Allie, what brings you to Nashville? Are you a country music fan?"

"I'm meeting some friends here, and you? What brings you to Nashville?"

"I'm here for a convention. Starting tonight you might see a lot of people in square dance clothes, especially near the Convention Center. I apologize in advance, but I'm going to have to eat and run."

"How quaint." She didn't ask why I had come to the convention, and I didn't feel the need to volunteer any details.

Our waitress came by and I ordered a hamburger, salad, and water. I decided to try a different tack. "Have you decided what you are going to do with the house? Do you plan on living there?"

"I'm afraid it only has bad memories now," she responded with an exaggerated sigh.

"So which realtor will you be using? The same one who sold you the house?" I was fishing, but she didn't know that I knew there was no sale.

"I just can't come to grips with it all." She evaded my questions and added, "I may just let some friends take care of business."

I tried to school my expression. I found her response a bit overdramatic and blasé at the same time.

"Allie, we never had a chance to talk. Where did you and Jake live before Isquith? Were you or he connected to Technocorp?" I reverted to basic small talk while I waited for my food. That was another interesting thing. She had waved off ordering, saying she'd already eaten. Judging from the waitress' expression, she hadn't eaten here.

"We lived wherever our jobs took us. Did you have another chance to talk to Jake? Is that why he was in your drive?"

I started at her question. Did she think Jake had been visiting me?

"No, I'm afraid the only time I spoke to either of you was when I brought the flowers over when you were moving in. I was out of town that day. I have no idea why he was in my drive. He didn't say anything to you about walking over?"

Now it was her turn to start. "Uh, no. I wasn't there either. I went out of town." She bristled a little. "You know that. I told you and that man."

That about ended my conversational skills and thankfully, my dinner arrived. I tried one more attempt to get her to talk while I ate. "Will you and your friends be going to Opryland or the Grand Ol' Opry while you're here?"

She smiled and with a tilt of her head answered, "I don't know. It will be a short visit." After looking around the restaurant, she leaned toward me as she added, "It's been nice chatting with you Darla. I'll see you around." With that she left the restaurant.

The waitress looked a bit bewildered and came over to the table. Chewing the inside of her cheek, she asked if the other lady was coming back. I shook my head and told her I didn't think so. "Will you be paying the check then?" she asked. My expression must have been priceless. She put her hand to her mouth and muttered something. I asked her to bring me the check. That seemed to placate her. It ended up that Allie had not only stressed me out but she'd stuck me with the bill! And apparently she had ordered appetizers and several drinks. I found out by asking the waitress that Allie had been sitting at the table since around 3 o'clock. She had told the waitress she was waiting for someone. I wondered if I was that someone.

A bit shaken and needing to get to the Convention Center, I went back to my room and picked out an outfit for the night. I decided I didn't like it and changed. Eventually, mostly because I ran out of time, I ended up with a green western style shirt, green and pink paisley scarf, and jean skirt. I locked everything except a small wallet and my phone in the room safe. Wallet and phone went in my pocket with my room key. I took the thumb drive I needed for the night and I was off.

I checked with the hotel concierge and he directed me to the shuttle to the Convention Center. Seeing some of the other dancers and callers got my mind off my dinner visit and raised my spirits. I always liked working with Tom and Slim Greenville, and Tom's wife Stacy was a lot of fun. We talked and laughed for the short ride. As we approached the mammoth building, the conversation toned down a bit. The bus driver let us out at the main entrance and there were signs directing everyone where to go for what. First stop, check in.

We all bustled through the door to numerous tables. One set for pre-registration, one set for on-site registration, one set for the vendors, and more tables for announcements and everything else. Slim, Stacy, Zach, and I went to the appropriate lines for pre-registered people. These tables were in the lobby itself. The other tables were in rooms against the wall behind us. As I moved forward in my line, I looked around. It was still an hour before the dance would begin, with a grand march set for 7:15 and dancing at 7:30. Yet, a lot of people were already milling around.

When it was my turn, the volunteer from the Nashville Regulars Square Dance Club handed me my official program and put a sticker on my name tag that would let the folks at the doors of the events for the next three days know I was paid up. The sticker sported a big "C" and the volunteer cheerily explained that was to let others know I was a caller.

She gave me directions to the room the callers and cuers were using to stage and organize the activities. Most square dance conventions include round dancing as well. Like square dance callers, round dance cuers tell dancers what movement to do next. One difference is that square dancers move in squares of four couples, and round dancers partner-dance and move around the room as a couple. The movement names differ, too, but a lot of dancers enjoy both square and round dancing.

With all the distractions and noise, I missed half her directions. I did what I usually do in these situations, and I found someone I knew was going to the same place. Bingo! Zach was just getting his stuff together. I walked in his direction and we set off to join the rest of the callers and cuers, or at least those who were working tonight. As far as I knew, only four callers were scheduled for tonight, each of us calling for about 30 minutes. In addition to Zach, Tom, and I, someone named Donnie McIntyre was calling. Checking the program quickly, it looked like Diana Richardson was the only cuer for tonight.

From the registration area in the lobby, we passed both entrances to the Central Exhibit Hall and entered the West Exhibit Hall. As we walked into the hall, on our right we saw vendors getting set up, display materials and merchandise being offloaded from the freight dock. Zach and I looked around and walked back out. I remembered the directions included a room in the Hall. Sure enough, there was a door with 101 on it at the doorway, but it was locked. We went in again and looked around some more.

One of the vendors, a nice looking man in western duds, must have noticed our lost look. "Where you two headed?" he asked.

"Trying to find the callers' room," said Zach.

"You're almost there," the man answered. He pointed to a room off the right of the hall. We thanked him and headed in. Slim, Tom, and Stacy were already there. The room wasn't shaped like a regular room and probably doubled for storage at times. Still, it would do. A pleasant looking woman was sitting there sipping water and reading the program. She introduced herself as Diana, the round dance cuer. We all sat down together to figure out the plan for the evening.

Although three halls would be used in some way during the convention, tonight only the Central Exhibit Hall would be used for dancing. Vendor booths, concessions, and other activities would be in the others. Friday and Saturday nights, with a larger crowd expected, East and Central would both be used for dancing, with the divider between them opened. Water and light refreshments would be at the far end of the East Hall along with flyers on various activities, upcoming dances, and a display on the history of square dancing. During the day, some of the workshops would be on the second floor. From the exhibit hall, we could look up and see where the rooms were located. East and Central Exhibit Halls would have the larger workshop groups for Mainstream and Plus levels of dancing. I didn't envy the hotel staff who would have to do all the setting up and rearranging.

For the time being, we limited ourselves with tonight's program to keep from getting overwhelmed. Slim would start out, then I would call, followed by Zach, and Donnie would bring it to an end. Diana would cue for 30 minutes before the squares started, and she'd cue one round dance in between tips. Slim liked to do harmony, and I knew he wanted to do a four-part harmony with all the callers for the close, but that would depend on Donnie. And Donnie wasn't here yet.

With everything taken care of, I decided to walk around and get my bearings for the rest of the weekend. I took the stairs to the second floor and started looking for the larger rooms where the line dancing, round dancing, and clogging workshops would take place. I was free during one of the line dancing ones and hoped to get a chance to brush up on my skills. Sometimes a club I called for wanted to have line dancing between tips instead of a two-step, polka, or waltz.

As I walked around I was happy to see that there was a reception area with information to help people find the rooms they wanted. The rooms looked to be good sized with plenty of space to move around. My phone vibrated, alerting me to a message from Paul. He hoped to arrive before the 7:30 start time and would meet me at the Convention Center. I texted back where I would be and let him know that I'd be calling between 8 and 8:30.

I decided to head downstairs and see if Donnie had arrived yet. I needed to mingle and be sociable with the dancers already gathering. And I wanted to check out the vendors on the way. I was looking for something in a prairie skirt length with a western print and top to match. With that thought in mind, I took the stairs closest to the lobby and stopped short when I stepped out of the stairwell. Allie stood against a nearby wall, scanning the people who came in the main door and those who come out of the elevators.

I knew there was no way Allie being at the Convention Center could be chalked up to coincidence. I mean, yeah, she could just happen to be meeting friends in Nashville. She could just happen to be in the hotel restaurant. No way does anyone "just happen" to be at a square dance convention. I watched her a moment, my mind churning. She was studying the crowd, apparently looking for someone. She turned while I still stood there staring at her.

"Hi Darla! After our little talk today, I decided to stop by and see what all the square dancing excitement is about. Will you explain what all this means for me?" She asked most innocently.

Politeness can go only so far, and this was pushing it. Still, I wanted to find out her motive for being here so I played along with what was obviously a ruse on her part.

"Sure, Allie. Let me give you the short version. The convention is Friday and Saturday, starting at noon tomorrow. Tonight there's a dance called a Trail End for those who wanted to come early and get a little extra dancing in. In about

15 minutes, everyone will meet up in the Central Exhibit Hall and the dance will start. There are chairs along the walls for those not dancing."

I wanted to grill her. I wanted to find out exactly what she had in mind. I knew if I pushed her too much, I wouldn't get straight answers. Better to let her take the lead and maybe I'd figure it out. I pulled out my phone and checked the time for show.

"Nice to see you, Allie. Glad you had time to stop by the convention. I have to run, since I'll be calling in a little while." I started to move past her, but she stopped me.

"Darla, I think I'll just walk with you. I may have some questions for you," she said. "I spoke with one of those ladies over there and she gave me this guest pass." That was odd. Most often such a pass would be given for someone who couldn't dance because of an injury but was with a dancer. I wondered just what she told those ladies.

"Sure," I replied with resignation. "I'm headed for a quick stop at the vendor booths, and you might enjoy seeing the things they have for sale."

That way I'd be where I needed to be and Allie might accidently spill some secrets on the way. I looked at skirts and shirts, or at least pretended to, and explained the specialty items to her as I browsed. My mind wasn't on shopping any more, though. It was racing. As Allie checked out shoes and clothes, she seemed a bit confused by the crinoline petticoats and the pettipants. With a number of vendors, the time went quickly. Next thing I knew, it was time to move to the Central Hall.

Zach texted me that we needed a quick pow-wow. Donnie still hadn't arrived. I apologized to Allie and told her I had to get to work.

"I'll come along," she said. Not a question, so I didn't reply. She could come if she wanted, maybe I'd be able to figure out her angle.

When I met up with the other callers, Allie was still in tow. They looked from me to her with questioning expressions. I shrugged but didn't introduce her. It was obvious that she was not a square dancer. Some square dance clothes, especially two-piece outfits or boots, are pretty pricey, but nothing compared to her designer digs and jewelry. She belonged on Wall Street, not at a square dance. Besides, I had no rational explanation for why she was there.

"Allie, go ahead and choose a seat against the wall, if you want to stay, that is. I need to do some business with these other entertainers," I said. She left reluctantly and looked in our direction frequently. We worked out a new program in case Donnie didn't show up in time to call his portion, and that was about all we had time for before the General Chairmen of the Convention, Gene and Jayne Joiner, tested the microphone and called for the dancers' attention. As people settled down, Gene asked if all dancers would line up in two lines of four, for a grand march. He stressed this was just to start out and get a quick count of the dancers. There would be no order for the march today, although at more formal dances the couples group with officers in the lead followed by club units. Tom, Stacy, Zach and I started one side. Two couples in state officer outfits took the lead on the other line of four.

Fairly quickly dancers lined up behind the leaders and on cue we clover-leafed and led each line around the side of the hall and back up to the center, keeping time to the lively music in the background. More dancers joined one or the other lines as they came in. Jayne took over at this point, muting the music and welcoming everyone to dance. She asked the two lines to form an aisle down the middle for the presentation of the colors.

Six individuals carrying the U.S. flag and the Tennessee flag marched down as she introduced their organization. Gene asked Slim to join him on the stage to lead the Pledge of Allegiance and national anthem, and the dancers rustled as they put their hands over their hearts. Together we recited the pledge and sang the anthem. Slim thanked Gene and Jayne, announced "Square 'em up!" and the dance began.

I danced the first tip with Zach and then walked around a bit. I hadn't heard from Paul again, so it looked like he wasn't going to make it before my turn at calling the dance. I was trying to be sociable as I chatted with folks who sat out the next couple of tips, but really I was scanning for Allie. Or Paul. I wasn't sure how the interaction would go between them, and I wanted to warn Paul before he saw her. I spotted Allie about the time that Slim started his third tip. That was my cue to get myself back toward the stage.

I grabbed some water, checked my phone for a text from Paul. None. I took time to send him a quick text of "Allie here, see me first" that I hoped wasn't too confusing for him. I jumped about a foot high when Allie tapped on my shoulder.

"So, are you going to perform now? I came to watch. I think Jake would have liked this." Her words conveyed wistfulness yet her tone carried a hint of aggression. I had no idea what her angle was. She was a good actress and, I'd decided, would be an excellent poker player. She didn't give anything away.

"That's right, I am going to be on stage next. I hope you enjoy the dance, Allie." I turned and walked away. The woman gave me the creeps.

When I got to the stage I made sure my music was ready to go and decided on a combination of my tried and true songs with one new thrown in. For the new one, I chose "I Hope You Dance." Soon enough, Slim called for a break and I was up. Slim and I chatted while we switched out thumb drives and the dancers took a break. Most headed for the water dispensers.

I got their attention with my own "Square 'em up" and I was immediately absorbed with the dance and dancers. As I am prone to do, I located my Clearton friends on the dance floor and tracked my choreography with them. It takes all my concentration to keep the squares moving, so I didn't have time to think about Allie or Paul or anything else.

At the two short breaks, I stayed on the stage and glanced around as I grabbed a quick drink. I spotted Allie the first break, but not on the second break. I didn't see Paul come in either. During my third tip, it seemed that Carlotta and Nick also left the dance floor. After the third tip, it was Zach's turn to call. As he prepared his music, Slim came up and said Donnie had shown up but wasn't interested in doing any harmony on the last song. That meant I was through with my calling obligations for the night. I collected my thumb drive and went in search of Allie, Paul, or Carlotta. My phone showed a text from Paul that simply said "here" so I knew he was somewhere at the convention.

When I got back toward the vendors, I saw Paul and he pulled me into his arms between the hanging racks of skirts. My immediate excitement was stifled when he whispered, "Do you know where she is now?"

I shook my head. Of all the nerve! He looked around and didn't seem to notice that I was put off by his unromantic greeting. I was surprised he couldn't see the steam coming off my head. I was about to say something sarcastic to him when Nick joined us.

"Darla, Paul. Carlotta followed that woman into the ladies room just now. The one in the lobby. Sorry we missed the rest of your tips, Darla. We've been following her since she left the Exhibit Hall." He raised one hand as he pulled out his phone and read the incoming text. "Okay, she's heading for the front door. What do I tell Carlotta?"

"Let's go," Paul said as he took off for the front of the building and the lobby. Unfortunately, by the time we got there, all Carlotta could tell us was that Allie had gotten on the shuttle back to the hotel. Our hotel.

Paul made an unidentifiable sound in his throat and finally really looked at me. I didn't say a word. Carlotta and Nick made excuses and went back in for the last part of the dance. There were after parties at each of the area hotels, but I wasn't in the mood.

"Is something wrong?" he asked.

"Are you kidding me? Yes, Paul, something's wrong," I answered. "You grab me, pull me into your arms, and then ask where Allie is?"

Paul had the grace to look a little shamefaced. "Sorry, Darla. Sometimes I just get into a case and get carried away. Let me try it again, okay?" He pulled me into his arms and kissed me with the obvious intent of letting me know how he felt. He succeeded, though I was still a little miffed and didn't see how this was his case in any way. Of course, I was the one who texted him so I was partly to blame, I guess.

The hotel shuttle returned and we boarded. Paul asked about the dance and all the Clearton gang as we rode back. It took time before I calmed down and realized I better enjoy my time with Paul whenever I could get it. At the hotel, I asked him if he had eaten yet and he suggested room service. Up in my room, he ordered food for both of us. When I had the chance to ask a question, I did.

"Paul, you said something about getting into a case? Did you mean Jake's murder? How did it become your case? Jake Carstairs was killed in my driveway. That's not a federal case." There, I had said it.

"Darla, it is a federal case. Jake and Allie Carstairs were in the witness protection program. His real name was Jackson Mendel. He and Allie, actually Glenys McCoy, met where they worked in Chicago. She was the secretary to the president of a large company. Turned out the company was a pyramid scheme and the president, Parker Schwindle, had stolen money from thousands of people who thought they were getting a good deal on some miracle retirement plan. Jackson was an accountant there. They both agreed to testify against the man and were put in the house next to you as a safe house. Guess it wasn't so safe. Jackson was killed before their handler could work out all the details."

"Wow. That puts a whole different slant on it. Okay, so why is Allie in Nashville and hanging out at a square dance?" I asked, a bit bewildered by his tale.

His jaw clenched. "We don't know. We don't yet know where she was the night he was killed. The handler said he never got a good feeling from her, felt that Jake-Jackson only was involved because of her, never felt that she was being honest."

"As far as I'm concerned they're Jake and Allie. The way you describe her, though, that would certainly go along with her behavior, which to me isn't exactly the grieving widow. What does that have to do with me? At the restaurant today, she implied that Jake had been at my house, visiting with me. She is a very odd lady."

"What do you mean 'at the restaurant' Darla?"

I related the tale of my dinner, her lying in wait for me, and stiffing me with the tab. I told him as much of the conversation as I could recall. In the meantime, our food arrived. As we ate, I commented on her last few words to me. I still didn't understand why she would be following me or why someone had broken into my house. It didn't occur to me to wonder how they ended up in the house next door in the first place.

As I puzzled on the questions, Paul took me in his arms again. Nope, we were not going to the after party downstairs.

Chapter 16

The next morning, we had a quick breakfast in the room and took the shuttle to the Convention Center. Paul and I walked up to the second floor where I was charged with my first Plus workshop. Thankfully, I shared this assignment with Slim who was an old hat at calling Plus moves. Plus dance moves are one level above Mainstream dancing, and while I was confident in calling some of the Plus moves I wasn't sure I was up to teaching all of them. I was nervous enough that I completely forgot about Jake and Allie. Paul did the pleasantries with Slim and immediately disappeared. Not interested in sticking around and watching me teach, I suppose.

Slim was in a good mood and teased me a bit about hanging out with someone who didn't square dance. Though that continued to be a bone of contention between Paul and me, I just laughed at Slim's teasing. We went through the Plus calls and decided which ones each of us wanted to cover. I hesitated and he was nice enough to let me pick the ones I was most comfortable with. That translated into which ones I had practiced for both a patter and singing call.

Dancers trickled in and soon we had four and then five squares. Any more and we'd have to see about a different room! It came out just about right, so we struck up the music and started the workshop.

Slim started us off, and he went through several of the simpler Plus moves. After that, he started work-shopping the move called "Follow Your Neighbor." It's a complicated move, and one I certainly didn't feel qualified to teach. Dancers start out holding hands in a box formation. Next, the two front dancers let go of their partners and step forward to the person across from them in the box. They join hands and do a three-quarter turn. The dancers following their "neighbors" finish up the move by doing a similar turn and fitting into the ends of the new formation. All in all, the dancers end up with their original partners but in a wave instead of a box formation.

While Slim instructed the dancers in the move, I watched the floor. Quite a few of the dancers already knew the movement and Slim's instructions simply served as reminders. Most of the squares were doing the move smoothly. Even so, Slim moved on to drilling it over and over. He would get them into the starting position and then call "Follow Your Neighbor!" The dancers would step forward, turn, and flow into a wave.

"Follow Your Neighbor!" he called out. And again, "Follow Your Neighbor!"

Bang. Just like that, my train of thought turned to my neighbor, dead Jake. And Allie, my "neighbor" who had apparently followed me to this convention. Could the square dance move help me figure out what was going on? Who were the 'dancers' in each box? My mind raced.

"Darla? Darla, you're up. What move did you want to teach?" Slim interrupted my thoughts, and I realized I'd spaced out for longer than I realized. Shaking myself back to the present, I smiled and took the microphone from him.

"Great job on that move, dancers. Now let's try a Teacup Chain, followed by a Beer Mug Chain!"

I heard groans from the dancers who knew what that meant. A Teacup Chain puts women dancers in the middle of the square and the men dancers don't have to do much work on the outer edges. There really isn't a square dance call named "Beer Mug Chain." The term is used when a caller puts the men in the center of the square instead of the women, and hilarity usually ensues. I worked with the moves and got the crowd smiling, and covered a couple of other calls. In no time the two-hour workshop was done.

I was exhausted and very glad I had the afternoon free. I was hoping for some down time. Despite my tangent of wondering if the Follow Your Neighbor dance steps could help me sort out the Jake and Allie mystery, deep down I was hoping that Paul hadn't found Allie. The idea that we might walk around downtown, take in some sights, and relax a bit without worrying about the Jake and Allie thing was very appealing.

I checked my phone and texted Paul to let him know I was done. He texted I should come down to the lobby. Bummer. I found him with Allie sitting in chairs in the lobby. So much for my hopes of a pleasant afternoon stroll.

Paul stood and took my arm, "Darla, look who I ran into down here?" He made it sound like a complete surprise.

"I hope you don't mind that I've been chatting with your guy down here while you worked," Allie said with a smirk. I got the feeling her comment was intended to make me jealous. Unfortunately for her, I knew he was a feebee and she didn't. Joke's on her.

"Not at all. Paul does get bored easily. Are the friends you were meeting square dancers, Allie?" I asked as innocently as I could manage.

"No, Darla, they aren't. They haven't arrived yet so I'm just killing time. I figured if Jake was interested in what you do and where you live, maybe I should find out what the draw was."

Paul's brows shot up, and then back down in a split second. My mouth dropped open and I had trouble getting words out. All things considered, I think I recovered quickly.

"Ah… I don't know what you're talking about. I already told you I didn't see Jake again."

She didn't respond but her look was snide. After a very awkward silence, I looked up at Paul for direction.

He put his arm around me and smiled a smile that never reached his eyes. He gave me a squeeze and a quick kiss before he added, "It was good to see you again, Allie. We'll see you later maybe. We have plans for lunch."

He propelled me away from her and out the door. Instead of taking the shuttle we walked a few blocks without saying a word and found a small restaurant. Once we were seated, Paul broke the silence.

"Darla, I want you tell me again about the break-in and what your house looked like."

"And I want you to tell me what you and Allie were talking about when I arrived. Who goes first?" I don't know why I was miffed that he was working on the case while I was working, too, but I was. So sue me.

"Come on, Darla. I was just pumping her for information, but she's a tough interview. That's why I need to know more about the situation."

I huffed a bit, then complied. I went through the mess in the living area, in the kitchen, each of the other rooms. I got stuck on the frozen peas again, but he had another question.

"Give it up on the frozen food, Darla. The police had to take everything that might be evidence. Might have fingerprints. You know the drill. So whoever did this, somehow stopped before doing much damage in the bedroom or master bath, the other bedrooms?"

"Well, yeah. It's just different when it happens to me, I guess. I figured he heard me drive in and then drive out or something else spooked him. But what would he have been looking for?"

"Putting together Allie's insinuations and your break-in, along with some monies missing from the company in New York, my guess is that Allie, and possibly one or more of her friends, think Jake hid money somewhere, and they're thinking somehow in your house. Maybe they think he was hiding it when they found him in your driveway. They might even think you're in on it."

When I jumped in startled response to his last comment, he reached out and took my hand across the table. "That's the only thing that makes sense. So now, why is Allie here?" He drifted away from me, lost in thought.

The waitress came over to take our orders and I had to say his name several times before his attention returned to lunch. While we ate, two guys and a gal took the stage and provided some musical background. They weren't great, but they weren't bad either, and they helped keep our conversation off Allie and Jake.

After we ate, I did get my afternoon walk with Paul after all. We walked around a bit and took a quick turn through the

Country Music Hall of Fame. We caught a cab back to the hotel. Paul said he had some business to attend to and I went to my room to rest up for calling that evening. I usually take the stairs, but I was tired so I opted for the dreaded elevator.

As the elevator doors opened, I felt my usual discomfort with getting into such a closed space. Discomfort escalated to fear and panic as someone's arm came around my neck and pulled me away from the elevator. I lost my balance and fell against him. I felt him almost topple and intentionally leaned harder to see if I could knock him over. No such luck. He didn't let go, if anything it seemed like the pressure on my throat was that much stronger.

"Cool it lady! If you cooperate you might not get hurt!" he sneered. He quickly jerked me into the nearby stairwell through the door marked fire exit.

I couldn't scream in a choke-hold. Once in the stairwell, he relaxed his hold a little. And we weren't alone. I found myself looking at his partner, a man a little taller than me, on the heavy side. He must have picked his clothes out based on what a gangster would wear in a bad movie. He was dressed in black and black, his shirt a little tight over his gut, a chain going from his belt buckle around his hip and into a back pocket. A matching gold chain adorned his neck. His hair looked like he'd cut it himself. Either he hadn't showered in days or he wore some awful aftershave. If not for the Beretta he was pointing at me, he would have looked comical rather than threatening. But then, there was the Beretta pointed at me and the other guy still keeping a choke-hold. I wasn't laughing.

I couldn't see the man behind me but now that we were on the lower landing of the stairwell, his hold was a little more relaxed. Thankfully, he didn't seem to avoid showers. But again, the way I was sweating …

"You know what we want, where is it? You want to live, you'll give us what we want."

I managed to get out, "I have no idea what you are talking about. Honest."

The arm at my throat jerked and the other guy's eyes sparked with anger. "Look lady, don't give me that crap.

Jackson was at your house and he musta given it to you to hold. Glenys wouldn't turn on us. But Jackson, he was something else. Mostly a wimp, when he got scared he did stupid things. Like taking the load. Like not telling us where he stashed it. See how that turned out for him?"

He moved a little closer, way too close for comfort. "So where is it?"

"Honest, I don't know what you are talking about. I only met Jake – Jackson to you – for about five minutes tops and his wife was right there. He didn't give me anything. Really." I had a sinking feeling he didn't believe me as his expression darkened.

He sneered again and asked, "So which leg shall I shoot first as encouragement?"

I heard the sounds of boots coming down the stairs, and voices. The guy with his arm around my throat spun me around and into the wall and they both took off at a run. He muttered something at me but I couldn't tell what it was. I landed on my rear and hit my head on the wall as he threw me around. My head was spinning, and I was still trying to get up when the people we'd heard reached me.

"Oh, my gosh, are you alright?" one of the men asked while the other one came to my other side. Both men looked to be in their thirties and athletic. The western wear and boots they sported suggested they might be going out for a night on the town in Nashville.

As they pulled me up, I answered, "I am now. You have no idea how glad I am that you took the stairs."

I was still dizzy and they escorted me to the lobby and a seat. Once I told them what happened, which I described as an attempted mugging, one of them went to get security. I thanked them again and told the security guard what had happened, again abbreviated. I didn't bother trying to explain Jake or Allie, but I did tell him the incident might be part of a larger case and whom he should call. I declined any medical care, although I did ask the security guard to go with me to my room.

He was very nice and even checked to be sure no one was in the room. It didn't look like anyone had been there either. I dropped onto the bed after making sure the deadbolt lock was set. I made sure my phone was close by in case someone tried to break in. I must have passed out soon after.

Next thing I knew someone was knocking on the door. I immediately panicked. Then I recognized Paul's voice calling my name. It took me a second to realize the key wouldn't get him past the bolt. I unlocked the door and let him in, locking the door behind him. He didn't look surprised or even ask me about it. As usual, he already knew. How did he find out things so quickly, all the time?

"You want to tell me about it? I got the condensed version you gave the guard from Detective Rodriguez."

He moved close and guided me back to the bed to sit down. I burst into tears and he held me until I calmed down.

With a deep breath, I asked, "So what is it that Jake hid somewhere that these goons think I have?"

"A couple million dollars maybe? We know how much the company scammed people out of, some of it's unaccounted for. Hard to tell how much is missing, or if only one person took it all. Glenys or Allie is the most likely, although she has denied it all along."

"Why didn't you tell me any of this earlier?" I asked.

"Would it have made any difference?" he responded. He sighed with frustration and added, "Darla, how do you end up in the middle of these messes?"

Like it was my fault a guy got killed on my driveway. I didn't dignify his question with an answer. I wanted to scream, 'I don't know, I just want it to stop!'

I had slept for almost two hours. Paul suggested we get some dinner before the evening dance. Oh no, the dance! I checked the time on my phone to make sure I wasn't running too late. With all the excitement, I almost forgot I had to call at the dance. I pointed out we needed to be back in time for the clogging exhibition and grand march. Paul rolled his eyes, but agreed.

We found a hole-in-the-wall diner and had a good meal, this time with somewhat mediocre entertainment. Paul filled me in a little on his afternoon. He had contacted the handler again to get more information on Allie's alibi and her so-called friends. He didn't know much but had tracked her reservations to New Jersey and back to Dallas.

An agent in New Jersey was checking on her background. So far he had turned up two low-life friends with prison records. Paul would have photos of them by tonight some time and, of course, he wanted me to see if I could identify them. I explained again that I never saw the one holding me so I'd be hard-pressed to ID him. I might be able to recognize Beretta Guy. We talked about some other stuff, finished our dinner and hustled back to the hotel. Paul made some calls. I changed quickly and we were back at the Convention Center in no time.

Chapter 17

Paul saw me safely into the Convention Center. There was a bustle of activity and the usual exchange of hugs among the square dancers. I spotted Carlotta and Nick as we entered the center ballroom. She waved at us and ran over. She was pumped up and immediately started talking nonstop about their afternoon, the callers, and their time in downtown Nashville. Her excitement was contagious. I found myself forgetting about Jake and Allie and the man with a gun. Well, at least I wasn't thinking about them all the time. I didn't mention the incident in the afternoon and neither did Paul.

Sam and Zoe came over when they saw us as well. Sam just about split his sides laughing at the stories Carlotta had of the famous celebrities she thought she saw at a distance. We all tended to agree that it was not likely that Garth Brooks or Alan Jackson was walking down the street without anyone but her taking notice. Teasing, Sam asked her if she'd seen Elvis, too.

We made our way to the bleachers and found seats. Sam put his towel and Zoe's bag on two chairs to save seats for Doug and Cassie. Paul looked at the towel and then at me quizzically.

I explained, "Many men carry a small towel like that on their belt. It's to wipe away sweat on their face or their hands. See, there's a square dance couple embossed in blue on the towel. Square dancing is a workout when you do it right!"

I started to say more, but conversation stopped when the emcee called for attention and introduced the Mighty Mountain Clogging Team. It felt odd to have all the Clearton gang here and not see Doug. As if in response to my thoughts, Doug and Cassie joined us before the cloggers started. The troupe was excellent, doing several numbers to a range of music from popular to country to rap, with changing combinations of dancers. Clogging required so much energy and coordination, I was impressed that they could do four selections. Everyone clapped along with the music and then applauded and whistled at the end, even Paul.

The emcee had barely started directions for the grand march before the stands started to empty out. Square dancers are always eager to start dancing. I didn't see Zach or anyone to partner with, so I hung out with Paul in the bleachers. He kept looking around even when I spoke to him. He finally turned and asked me about the schedule for the night. I showed him in the program when I would be calling. I was in the main ballroom with Mainstream and announced Plus dancing tonight. I had three tips to call, one each hour. He squeezed my shoulder and whispered, "Try to stay with people. Follow the usual female tradition and go to the restroom with someone, will you?"

I nodded and asked, "Where will you be?"

He shrugged. "I'm gonna walk around the lobby here and at the hotel, and come back over here. Maybe I'll run into our friend Allie again."

We stood on cue for the presentation of the colors and national anthem, and then he left. I moved down to floor level and chatted with people who were sitting out the first tip. I saw some dancers I'd met at the Texas Federation Festival last month and was oh so glad for nametags!

I grabbed some water and a piece of cake, and thought about running to the restroom before my time on stage. After the current caller and a break, I would be up. I spotted Carlotta and asked her if she wanted to join me. She immediately became alert and, if it was possible, even more keyed up, and said "of course." Despite Paul's reference to 'female tradition,' it was an odd request from me and she asked what was up.

On the way, I gave her the short version. She wanted the long version, but there just wasn't time. We returned to the ballroom and I moved toward the front. Max, the caller finishing up, and I exchanged greetings, hugs, and places on the stage. Sticking to the schedule, at 7:45 I gave the call, "Let's dance!"

I started with a favorite of mine I could call in my sleep and the crowd seemed to like, "Margaritaville." I followed it with "Ridin' my Thumb to Mexico," a song I knew was one of Doug's favorites. I looked for him and Cassie, I guessed they must have gone to the Plus Only ballroom. In no time, I was changing places with Zach and on my own for an hour.

As Zach prompted dancers that he was about to start, Sam came by and asked if I had a partner, explaining Zoe wanted to sit this one out. I agreed, appreciative of the opportunity to dance and suspecting Zoe was graciously sitting out to give me a chance to dance. I whispered to Sam that I was pretty sure that Zach would do "Calendar Girl." As the music started, both Sam and I chuckled and high-fived.

While most square dancers like variety in their dance music, they don't mind hearing old favorites. Each dance is different because you're dancing with a different set of dancers in your square. Zach did another Neal Sedaka number and soon enough it was break time again. Sam and I walked over to Zoe and I thanked her for loaning him out. She laughed and commented, "You need to get your man to square dance, Darla, or you need to get yourself another man!"

I didn't have a quick or diplomatic answer. Thankfully, Sam whisked her onto the dance floor to finish the two-step playing. Her comment made me think about Paul and I looked around to see if he was handy. Zoe had a point. It was hard to not feel slighted when he didn't even stay to hear me call or seem to have any interest in learning to square dance despite the teasing of my friends. I gave myself a shake and smiled as Carlotta and Nick walked toward me.

"Saw you got to dance at least one tip, Darla!"

"Yeah, Zoe loaned out Sam. It was fun. Great crowd don't you think?" I asked.

Carlotta answered, "There have to be four thousand people here!"

Nick, always a numbers guy, looked a bit skeptical and asked, "Does anyone have an official count of the people who registered?"

"I'm sure they do. The Nashville Federation probably has those numbers. I can barely count squares from the stage, and with three ballrooms, and not everyone dances... I have no idea how many are in attendance."

We chatted a bit more. Carlotta had told Nick about my being grabbed by some thugs and he asked about it. As with Carlotta, I downplayed it. As we talked, one of the men who had helped me on the stairs recognized me and came over to ask how I was doing.

"I didn't realize you were a square dancer," I said. "Either way, I really appreciated your help. Thanks so much."

"Glad we were there to help. I didn't realize you were a caller, either, but I sure enjoyed your tip. Catch you later!" He chalked the incident up to a mugging and I let him.

The rest of the night I noticed that Carlotta and Nick seemed to stick close by. I spotted Paul once while I was calling and almost lost track of where I was in the song. By the time I finished, he'd disappeared again. I didn't see Doug and wondered to myself why I kept looking for him. As Slim called the last tip, I started to get antsy. I hoped I could get Paul to go to the after party tonight. It was the 'official' one and was hosted by the Nashville Federation. It would be fun, but as a caller it would be job-related for me as well.

As the square dance ended, Slim prompted everyone to attend the party. A local country western group was scheduled to provide the entertainment. The emcee thanked all the local clubs who were providing refreshments and then reminded everyone that the party was BYOB. Alcohol and square dancing don't go together so dances don't include alcohol. After parties, well, that was a whole other matter. I checked my phone and texted Paul he could find me at the party.

I joined the Clearton group, but opted to keep to water. Sam chastised me for not telling him I'd been mugged and I assured him I was fine. No keeping secrets among the Clearton gang, apparently.

"You know there's never time to talk when we're dancing," I said. To change the subject, I asked if anyone knew the band that would be playing at the after party. I hoped they were good, although if Paul didn't show up I likely wouldn't get to dance to them. We all got snacks and settled in as we waited for the band. Two men and two women took the stage. In no time they were playing country songs we all knew and loved.

As they started Billy Currington's "Must be Doin' Something Right," I felt a hand at my back. I jumped from the touch before I realized it was Paul. He pulled me onto the dance floor after he apologized for scaring me. He held me close and his hand played across my back, inconspicuously I hoped, while we danced. His moves went right along with the words of the song. He was doing something right.

We danced and socialized for a while and bid my friends good night. I hadn't spotted Allie all night. Paul had only seen her from a distance as she left the Convention Center and got into a cab. He was too far away to get a cab number and the cab traffic at this large a convention center made it impossible to track down where she went.

Chapter 18

I woke in the morning alone in the room and hopped into the shower. I was out and getting dressed when Paul knocked softly and let himself in. He had coffees and breakfast for us. Who could complain about that? He gave me a quick kiss and then we both ate and read the paper. As I finished and put the paper down, I saw Paul watching me.

"Did you enjoy your breakfast, Darla?"

"Yes, thank you! And you?" I started to feel a little awkward. Something was about to happen.

"Can we talk about Allie for a bit?" He continued without waiting for me to answer. "I already mentioned the witness protection and pyramid scam Schwindle was pulling and that we think Allie stole millions. Part of the money has been located in a bank in Grand Cayman, but there's still a huge chunk of change not accounted for. Pretty obvious the guys who threatened you and Allie think Jake took part of the cache. I think it's also pretty clear they think he gave it to you or hid it at your house. Are you with me on this?"

"Paul, I get it. I realize that's what Allie and the thug with the gun think. Like I keep telling you and Rodriguez, I only talked to Jake for less than five minutes at their house with Allie standing there. I gave them a vase of flowers. Don't you believe me?" I was getting irritated very quickly.

"Darla, I believe you. I also believe that truth or fiction, Allie and those men don't believe you. You are in danger unless we can identify the men and somehow snare Allie." His voice had gotten louder and as he finished he punched the table. I wasn't sure if it was keeping me out of danger or catching Allie that was causing his reaction.

As he ran his hands over his face and into his hair, he let out a deep breath. "I'm sorry Darla. I'm worried about you and this case is making me crazy." At least equal parts, I hoped. He reached for my hand and I let him take it, but there was no warmth on either end.

"There's more, isn't there?" I asked. He looked down at the table as he spoke.

"I mentioned some lowlifes Allie was associating with. Are you up for looking at some mug shots? Possibly identifying the man whose face you saw?"

I shook my head. "Paul, I'm sure I can't identify the one who had me in the choke-hold. I never saw his face. I might be able to identify the one I could see. I know it was a Beretta he was pointing at me, like straight out of Lethal Weapon. So do we go back to Isquith? I'm supposed to be calling at a workshop this afternoon and I'm scheduled for a half hour." A bit wistfully, I added, "I hoped to have some time to relax, see a little of Nashville, maybe spend some time together." I watched fleeting expressions cross Paul's face as I spoke. I couldn't identify any of them. He leaned forward.

"We can go to the FBI office here in Nashville before your workshop, and maybe take in some sights. What time is your workshop?"

I guessed it was good he had at least heard part of what I said. We bartered back and forth on the schedule, and I managed to win on checking out the Country Music Hall of Fame and Museum before our visit to the FBI office. I knew that once he got "on the case," I'd be second fiddle.

We cabbed it downtown and toured through the Artifact and Photograph Collections. The costumes and other items in the Artifact Collection were impressive. Some of the cars and microphones, the various old musical instruments were cool to see. The collections showed the history of country music and musical entertainment in general.

I could tell Paul was getting tense and we didn't check out any other exhibits. Another time. Paul would have skipped lunch, but I convinced him to grab a quick bite before he flagged another taxi and directed the cabbie to the FBI office. I enjoyed the morning, but found myself tensing up even in the car. As we entered through the building's security screenings, I remembered that I'd become a square dance caller to avoid these kinds of situations.

Paul put his arm around my shoulder as we walked down the quiet halls. I knew he was trying to comfort me, but it was more like he was pushing me along. I almost wanted to blame him for this whole mess, and forced myself to shake off the thought. This was not his fault. Whether he had pulled strings to be assigned to the case or not, it was his job. I rolled my shoulders to relax. He looked at me with raised eyebrows.

We stopped at a nondescript door, and Paul knocked and opened it before anyone answered. He introduced me to the agents in the office. After exchanging greetings, we went into a cubicle and sat down. Paul pulled out a large notebook and opened it up.

"Here you go, Darla. Take a deep breath and try to relax. See if you can spot the guy with the Beretta. I'll go grab us a couple bottles of water."

I nodded and he walked away. I could hear hushed talking in the larger room followed by quiet. I was glad Paul hadn't stayed to look over my shoulder. I closed my eyes for a few minutes and tried to visualize the man's face. I started through the notebook. About five pages in, I hesitated. I used my left hand to hold that page while I continued to turn pages. I finished the book and returned to the photo that looked familiar. I was beginning to wonder where Paul had gone to get the water, when he returned. He opened a bottle and handed it to me, opening his and taking a swig while he waited for whatever I had to say.

"I can't be sure, but I think this is the man with the Beretta in the stairs. See the tats here on his neck? I remember thinking they didn't go with his gangster motif."

"Come on, let's see what I can find out." He took the book from me and walked into the main part of the room to one of the computer stations. He pulled a chair over for me and went to work. The man's name was Jean Meurtrier. He and a few others were known associates of Schwindle and Allie. He had three registered firearms, including a Beretta. Guess I'd done good.

I almost sensed Paul's body start to sizzle with excitement. He yelled to the other two men, who came right over.

"What the hell are you doing, Harbinville? You know she can't see the database. Heaven help us if this case goes to court." The one who spoke was a little red in the face, the other one just stone-faced.

"My goal is to keep Darla safe. You guys got a problem with that?" Paul challenged them. When no one answered, he explained that he needed to get me to the Convention Center and he'd meet them at the local address on file as soon as he could. Everyone except me was moving quickly as I watched the other two strap their guns on.

Paul took my arm with "Come on, Darla, no time to waste" as he propelled me out of the office and the building, and flagged down a cab. He left me at the Convention Center with another prompt to stick to the crowds or at least my friends. With a quick kiss, he was gone.

I knew I should be relieved that this "mystery" might be over soon, but I was keyed up. All that testosterone and adrenalin was contagious. I wandered around and ran into Carlotta and Nick.

"Darla, aren't you calling later on?" Carlotta asked.

"I call at 3 o'clock. I think it's the last tip of the afternoon. Why?"

Carlotta's mouth opened and closed, but no words came out. With some hesitation, she said, "Darla, you know that's just 30 minutes from now? Do you have clothes to change into?"

I realized then why she was hesitating. Here I was in jeans and a t-shirt, not exactly dressed as a performer. I was still processing my clothes crisis when she grabbed my arm and dragged me to the vendor area.

"Okay, so the jeans will work. We need to find you a western shirt. Something with a little bling!" She had a glint in her eye and I was a little afraid to see what she was going to come up with. "You might need a new pair of boots, too. What a pity!"

With a smile, Carlotta was in her element. She tore through the racks of tops while I tried to collect myself. First off, I assured myself that I had my credit card, so I could pay for this shirt with bling. At the same time, I was relieved to realize my thumb drive was still in my small wallet from the night before.

As time ticked by, Carlotta dragged me and three shirts to the dressing room and told me to pick one and hurry! I saw Nick chuckling behind her and just shook my head at him. In the dressing room, I selected the shirt with a paisley yoke and gold trim. The paisley was blues and purples. Thankfully, my belt was navy, so that worked.

I managed to get the shirt paid for, my t-shirt in a bag, and be in my place on the stage in 30 minutes, with about two minutes to spare. Close, too close. I owed Carlotta big time. I rolled my shoulders back and called out "Square 'em up!"

Two tips later, with a Grand Right and Left to end the afternoon, I walked off the stage. Carlotta, Nick, Sam, and Zoe gave me hugs and we all headed to the exit to catch the shuttle to the hotel. I hadn't heard from Paul and didn't know if they had arrested Meurtrier yet. Carlotta asked where Paul was and I explained that he was looking for the person who mugged me. At the hotel, Carlotta told Nick to go ahead to their room, that she and I were going to have some "girl time" before dinner.

Carlotta and I kept the conversation light. For her part, she decided to help me choose my clothes for the final dance of the convention. I was only calling two tips in the Mainstream hall, but she was gung ho on choosing my outfit. Unlike Carlotta, I tend to go for the longer prairie skirts or even the flared skirts that are just as much western wear as square dance duds.

She picked out the black tulip flared skirt I brought because it reminded me of the video of John Michael Montgomery's "Grundy County Auction." She selected a black, blue, and white peasant shirt to go with it. Next came the makeup and her feeble attempt to get my hair to do something besides just bob. I'm not usually into makeup but Carlotta kept me laughing and certainly kept my mind off the mugging and murder and mystery.

When I was dressed and dolled up to Carlotta's satisfaction, we went down to her room. Nick gave me a wolf whistle and told Carlotta to get moving. She looked fresh and ready in less than 10 minutes. Amazing. We connected with Sam and Zoe in the lobby. Doug joined us and the expression on his face was every bit as flattering as Nick's whistle. Sam asked if we should wait on Cassie, but Doug explained she was tired and might join us at the dance later.

We went to the steak house next door for dinner. Although initially awkward with Doug, I found myself relaxing and feeling comfortable as always with the Clearton gang. Other than a few remarks and questions about "my mystery" most of the conversation was about the callers, the workshops, new songs, and great food. Before long it was time to head to the last dance of the convention.

Doug and I partnered up for the Grand March and the first tip. He disappeared after that for the first few tips. After my time on stage, he was waiting. Alternating with rounds, country music was played between tips. We waltzed and as the song ended, my phone vibrated. Following the text message directions, I turned around and Paul walked over to us. Doug thanked me for the dance and walked away.

Paul and I walked out to the lobby area and found a quiet corner to talk. As he took me in his arms, he whispered, "Sorry it took so long."

We sat down as he continued, "Well, we got Meurtrier and a friend of his who was at the house. We spent the last three hours trying to get him to talk. He implicated Allie in syphoning off some of the money from Schwindle. He admitted, somewhat reluctantly, to grabbing and threatening you. 'Course that was after we told him his pal had sold him out. It wasn't true, of course, but it worked. We got him from your ID. From what he told us, Allie figured out that Jake had taken some of the money she'd stashed in the all the packing materials."

"So did he kill Jake? And where's the money? And how did they end up in that house?" I knew I was rattling off too many questions at once, but I had all these questions bouncing around my head.

"He gave us more than we thought he would. He admitted to killing Jake once the death penalty was taken off in exchange for information on Allie/Glenys. Jake refused to tell them where he put the money even when threatened. According to Meurtrier, he bumped Jake with the car as a threat and when Jake wouldn't talk he got so mad he shot him on the spot. To cover his tracks, he decided to run him over, as a last ditch effort in misdirection."

"Did he think that would hide a bullet?" I couldn't fathom that level of stupid.

He nodded with a chuckle and took my hand. "As for the house. That one is easy. The federal government needs to have "safe houses" across the nation in otherwise "normal" neighborhoods with little to no crime. With the balloon mortgage fiasco, the government quietly acquisitioned a house here and there in foreclosure. Not too many and none in within 500 miles of another. Then if they need to relocate someone with a new identity, it is easy for them to just move in and establish that new identity. Not everyone has your natural curiosity or would check to see if a recent sale occurred. The sale would have occurred six months ago or a year ago. When the federal government buys a house, there's not always a record of it."

I nodded and realized that made sense. Yup, just a little too much curiosity. Not the first time I'd heard that. To Paul, I asked, "Okay, so where is the missing money?"

"A very good question. From what Meurtrier told us, Allie had it all hidden in with the packing materials during the move. It seems Jake must not have liked having the money around. It scared him. Somehow in the unpacking, he hid it. She left and was supposed to pay the lowlifes for covering her theft, but by then she already knew some of the money was missing. The only indication that he went anywhere is that he ended up in your driveway. A very short timeframe to account for, Darla."

"Is it possible that Jake didn't hide the money, and she is lying through her teeth, blaming him? I don't trust her at all. Nothing about her rings true."

"You've got that straight! If that's the case, why is she following you? Going to extremes for a charade, don't you think? Why not just disappear to Grand Cayman where the rest of her money is. She has a passport. Meurtrier and his pal don't, so they certainly wouldn't follow her."

Somehow this all had to come together. In my world, things made sense. So far, this didn't. Paul told me to stay put while he checked the lobby and main hall. I tried to wrap my head around Jake's murder, the pyramid scheme, Allie, and Meurtrier. This all started with Schwindle pulling a con with Meurtrier as his muscle, Allie as his secretary, and Jake as accountant.

If I thought about it in square dance choreography, Allie started as partners with Jake, but took the arm of Schwindle and with his turning ended up as greedy as him. Jake followed her and rejoined her in witness protection. Meurtrier followed Schwindle and was left looking for the money. So I had half of the Follow Your Neighbor movement with Meurtrier, Schwindle, Allie, and Jake moving from a box formation to end up in a wave. In my head, they were the right-hand box. That was just the beginning.

I visualized a second box formation, at a later point in time. Somehow Allie and Meurtrier got the idea that Jake connected with me and turned. Allie followed me while Meurtrier followed, and killed, Jake. I gasped when I realized I had somehow become part of this second version, the left-hand box of Follow Your Neighbor. If I didn't get myself out of the wave, I could get killed. Allie was the only one left from the first wave, so that meant…

In the middle of choreographing "my mystery" in square dance terms, Paul returned. He didn't look happy, but he also didn't look worried.

"No sign of Allie. Don't worry, she's just a small fry in this thing."

"No, she's not! Paul, it's coming clear. She's the key to the whole thing! Meurtrier was only trying to find the money to get paid, by Allie! She's trying to find the money because she is greedy. I don't even think she'd have really paid

Meurtrier if she had the money. I don't think she cared one bit that Jake got murdered. She is cold and pathological, she might have even done him in herself if Meurtrier hadn't lost his temper and done the job before her."

Paul seemed to discount what I said, still he couldn't disregard it completely. It made too much sense. "If that's the case, then she might still think you have this money or know where it is. Let me check with the office here and see if they have located her."

I sat back and waited while Paul walked a few feet away to check. He came back and let me know that an APB had been issued for her, but so far no one had spotted her. It was getting late, and I was too tired to even suggest an after party. As we rode back to the hotel, Paul commented, "So, I saw you dancing with Weathers. What's with that?"

I was a bit taken aback. "He asked me to dance. No big deal." I wanted to add that at least Doug was around, but I bit my tongue. Besides, I'd been begging Paul to learn to square dance and he chose not to. Tomorrow, we'd all be heading home. When Meurtrier, his pal, and Allie were in jail, life might just get return to normal. Then we could talk.

Despite my rising concern over being in danger, and my less life-threatening conflicted feelings about Paul and Doug, I managed to get to sleep. The Clearton gang gathered in the lobby Sunday morning and shared a cab to the airport. Paul and I had said our goodbyes earlier in the morning, and he promised to call when he had any updates. Our little group was a lot quieter on the flight back to Dallas. It had been a tiring few days and we were all spent. And no Allie sightings on the return flight.

I drove home from Dallas and felt my anxiety mounting as I pulled in the driveway. I looked at the house next door, the one the Carstairs had moved into, and scowled. As I grabbed my bag to go inside my phone rang. It was Heather, a very welcome distraction to get me into the house. We chatted for a bit, and I sensed she wanted something but was hesitant to ask. I told her to call if she thought of anything she needed or if there was anything she wanted to tell me.

I managed to get the laundry going and called my sister. As usual, Julia talked about her life and never thought to ask about mine. Another nice distraction for now.

I sat down to watch television and decided it was hopeless. I was just too tired and my head was filled with conflicting emotions. Why and how had I become the focal point of this crime wave? What was going on with Doug and Cassie? What was going on with Paul and me? I opted out of the whole mess and went to bed.

Chapter 19

I woke with a start, dream images merging with reality. A huge dragon breathed fire at me and belched smoke while a crow circled above, screeching incessantly. As I surfaced, I realized the smoke was real and the crow was my smoke alarm. I rolled out of bed, grabbed my purse from the back of its chair, and headed toward the bedroom door.

When I stepped into the hallway, I ran into a wall of smoke that made me gag. Acrid singed-plastic odor assaulted me. Dropping my purse, I ran to the bathroom and grabbed a towel. I soaked it with water and tied it around my face like a bandit. Back in the bedroom, I saw the smoke was thicker. At this point, I could barely make out the doorway. Dropping to my hands and knees, I crawled toward the door.

I made it through the door of the bedroom, but after that the smoke was a total blackout. I took a moment to visualize the layout, but I was disoriented. Remembering my disaster training, I crawled along the wall feeling my way toward an opening. I thought I was headed toward the side window, or possibly the front door. I felt the carpet change to tile under my hands, and I knew I was near the front door. Then everything went black.

The next thing I knew, I was on the ground with an EMT urging me to wake up. She asked me to take several deep breaths while she listened to my lungs. She did a thorough checkup and recommended I take an ambulance ride to the emergency room. As usual, I stubbornly refused to go to the hospital. Physically, I knew I'd be fine. Emotionally, I wasn't so sure. She tried again. When she saw I wasn't budging she gave up. After checking my eyes, pulse, and breathing one more time, she returned to the vehicle.

Shaking, I sat down on the curb facing away from the house. I heard the shouts of the firefighters and the hiss of water against flames. Red and blue lights flashed up toward the main road, and a patrol car created a barrier on the other side of me. Other than emergency personnel, I was alone.

Neighbors had gathered just outside the perimeter and in the cul-de-sac, and I could hear Jeanette's voice over the others. "We're her neighbors! We need to see her!" I heard a murmur in response but couldn't tell what the patrolman told her. She wasn't persuasive enough to get through. I was just as glad. I wanted time to recover before I saw anyone.

Apparently, it didn't matter what I wanted, as I saw Paul headed my way. I no longer wondered how he found out about things, he just did. I took a deep breath and ran my hand through my hair. Lost cause.

"Darla, thank God you're okay," he said, pulling me up to give me a hug and a quick kiss. "Have the police interviewed you yet?"

I shook my head but couldn't form words yet.

"I'll go see what's holding them up," he said. "I'll be right back." No, he wouldn't. He'd get hung up finding out about the fire and I'd be lucky to see him in less than an hour. I held him on to him, unwilling to let him go.

I found my voice. "Would you just stay here a minute?" I asked.

"Are you hurt? I can get you something if you need it," he said.

"I need you," I said.

"And you will have me. Just as soon as I figure out what's going on here. Really, I'll be right back, Darla." I was attracted to his confidence and take-charge attitude, but right now it wasn't what I needed.

"Can I have your phone?"

He hesitated, then unhooked it from his belt and handed it over. The phone in my hand felt like a lifeline and I was less alone. I wanted to call Heather but knew I would just worry her. I stared at the phone, then my house. All I saw was black smoke against the breaking dawn. I hugged myself, and the phone felt cold where it touched my arm. I knew the person I wanted to call. The irony of calling Doug on Paul's phone wasn't lost on me, even in my current mental state.

I dialed his number and heard his gruff "hello." Forgetting he wouldn't see my name in his caller ID, I blurted out, "My house. A fire. "

"What? Darla? Is that you? Did you say your house is on fire?"

"Yes." Tears started rolling down my cheeks.

"My God. Where are you? Are you okay?"

"I'm home. My yard." I had trouble making complete sentences. The words came out disconnected.

"I'll be right there. I'm going to hang up now, okay? I'll get dressed and be right there," he said.

"Okay." I stared at the phone again and finally just slipped it into the pocket of my sweats. I sat down on the curb and let my head fall into my hands. I sat there for what seemed like hours. I'd thought it was all over once I identified Jake's killer. Why was this nightmare continuing? And why did I want to see Doug right now?

Still in that position, I was starting to feel better when Wayne and Jeanette broke through the line and made their way over to me. They sat on the curb on either side of me. Jeanette put her arm around my shoulders. Wayne took my hand, placed it on his knee, and started patting it. Neither of them said a word for a while. I felt their strength streaming into me.

"You guys are the best," I said. Wayne patted my hand a little harder and Jeanette leaned over and kissed my cheek.

"We're just so sorry this happened to you. You'll come stay at our house until you get things worked out."

It was a command, not an invitation, and I didn't question it. I just nodded and strangled out, "Thanks."

They were still with me when a policeman came over. I didn't know how long I'd been sitting there, not saying anything and barely thinking anything. He stood in the street in front of me and spoke up.

"Ma'am? Are you up to answering a few questions?" he asked.

"Can they wait?" I replied.

"Not really, ma'am. I need to get the facts down right away." He looked down at his tiny clipboard, the kind traffic cops carry. I doubted he needed the reminders, but I appreciated his official tone.

"Do you know where the fire started?" I told him I didn't.

"Do you know what might have started it?" I told him I didn't.

"Do you smoke?" I told him I didn't.

"Where were you when you first noticed the fire?"

"Asleep. My smoke alarm went off," I answered.

"Do you have any information regarding the fire you think we should know in our investigation?" he asked. I thought about that one.

"Officer, I don't know how much you know about the situation. There's an open murder investigation that might be related. Have you talked with Detective Rodriguez?"

That got his attention. He looked up from his clipboard.

"Detective Rodriguez?"

"Yes sir. He should be able to fill you in. I don't know if there's any connection or not," I said.

He had a few more questions. Unfortunately I had no more answers. I didn't distract him with any of my suspicions. For one thing, I wasn't really thinking straight. For another, I knew the fire investigation would turn up the facts of the fire. For yet another, I knew Paul was in touch with Rodriguez and Johnson. Anything I had to say would only be an opinion. Eventually, he felt he had done his job and he left.

I didn't see Doug break through the barrier at the end of the road, but one way or the other he managed to. Before I saw him, I heard him.

"Darla! Look at me, Darla. Are you okay?"

My legs were still shaky and I struggled to stand. Jeanette stood up and pulled me to an upright position. I barely caught my balance before Doug enveloped me in his arms. It felt wonderful. I sagged against him. With his hand behind my head, he pushed my face gently into the crook of his shoulder. Finally, I stopped smelling smoke and just smelled him. I thought he would never let me go, and I was fine with it.

Eventually he did, though. He stepped back and held me with both hands on my upper arms. His gaze locked with mine and held.

"Darla, you drive me crazy. Crazy with worry, crazy with frustration, crazy with jealousy." He hesitated. "Crazy with love."

In the deep recesses of my brain, the part that always tells the truth, I knew I had my answer.

"Sorry," I said.

He barked out a short laugh and pulled me to him again.

"Not the response I was hoping for, but I'll take it," he said.

"Doug, it's not that simple. We need to talk," I mumbled into his ear.

"It's that simple for me," he said softly. "And yes, we need to talk." His voice dropped even lower and I wasn't sure if he was talking to me or to himself. "But not now. Now I just need to have you in my arms," he said, and held me tighter. I put my face against his shoulder and breathed him in.

Eventually, a fireman came over to talk to me. He told me I couldn't go into the house for eight hours. Officer Johnson, who materialized sometime after the fire department arrived, cordoned off the house and told me she'd let me know when I could go in.

After the break-in, the police had posted an officer to watch the house until I returned from the hotel, but I couldn't expect them to continue acting as my personal security force. It was past dawn by the time the last emergency vehicle pulled out. I saw that a patrol car had stayed to watch the house. I went over to ask him how long he would be here. He said the forensics crew would start their work as soon as the fire department was sure there were no remaining hot spots and released the house. He would stay until then to make sure no one tampered with anything in the house. Doug offered to stay and watch the place, too, but I knew he had things he needed to do.

"I'm sorry I woke you up, but I'm not sorry I called you," I told him. "The officer will be here until the police get here, so the house is as secure as possible for now. You don't need to stay. Go take care of things and I'll see you later."

"We gotta talk," he said.

"I know. I'm not up to it now," I replied.

"Soon. I mean it," he said.

I just nodded.

After he left, I searched for Paul and found him talking with Officer Johnson.

"Darla! How are you holding up?" he asked, giving me a sideways hug. "Where are you staying tonight?"

"Not too good," I replied to his initial question. "And I'm staying with Jeanette and Wayne tonight. Where will you be?"

"I hadn't really thought about it yet. I'll get a room somewhere and talk with you in the morning." He really looked at me for the first time. "You need to get some sleep," he said.

Yeah, I did. I also needed some support from him, but I was too tired and confused to ask for it. Instead, I just gave him a quick kiss, handed him his phone, and took the opportunity to go with Jeanette and Wayne to their house. Jeanette ushered me to their guest room and I collapsed on the bed. This was going to be a helluva week coming up.

Chapter 20

Jeanette and Wayne were both up when I woke a few hours later. By mid-morning I had downed a couple cups of Wayne's excellent coffee, bolted down a cinnamon roll fresh from Jeanette's oven, borrowed a jacket from Wayne, and was headed for my house. Bless my wonderful neighbors. They wanted to come with me. I told them I would rather face it on my own. I wasn't sure how someone dealt with something like this, but I was about to find out.

Officer Johnson wasn't in evidence but there was lots of activity. I poked my head into the front door, which was still in place thank heavens, and asked who I should talk to. A young man in coveralls walked up.

"Tom Ferrar, ma'am. What can I do for you?"

"Tom Terrific, we call him!" came a shout from behind him.

"Can it, guys!" he shouted over his shoulder, and then turned back to face me. "It's been a long morning. Sorry," he said.

"No problem. Long one for me, too," I said. "I'm the owner. I really want to see the damage. Can I come in?"

After verifying a few confirming details, he accepted my statement and let me into the house. The damage wasn't nearly as bad as I had thought. It looked like someone sent something like an old-fashioned Molotov cocktail in through the side window, although all the windows were shattered so it was hard to tell. Tom Terrific looked at me with intense eyes and said that an attack like this was generally a warning. An arsonist could have easily burned the house down. Not a comforting thought. I'd wonder what the warning was later.

I walked around the living room, stunned. Apparently the overwhelming smoke I encountered came when the furniture caught on fire and from the burning electronics. My CDs formed a melted modern sculpture in the corner, and the stereo system and television would never work again. The floor was completely burned out in the middle of the room, so I had been right to follow the wall around last night. It looked like someone had held a campfire in the middle of the room.

The living room was pretty well destroyed from the fire, smoke, and of course water. As I followed Tom Terrific around, I noted that the rest of the house didn't look all that bad. The smoke smell followed us everywhere, and some of the walls were blackened. I blinked back my tears when I realized that the framed picture of Heather from her high school graduation had been destroyed.

"Did you find my purse?" I asked.

"I believe so," he answered. "On the kitchen counter, we've started a pile of items we've examined. It should be there."

I followed him into the kitchen and was relieved that the fire damage hadn't come this far. Sure enough, my purse was piled in a neat stack of other items on the counter.

"May I take it?" I asked.

"Yes, ma'am. We've photographed and examined everything, and the items in this pile are cleared. However, please don't take anything without letting us know. Ellen!" he called into the living room. A woman in matching coveralls came into the kitchen.

"Ellen, please take a photo of..." he hesitated and I could tell he was searching his memory before he continued, "...of Ms. King with her purse. She's taking it with her."

Ellen stepped back and snapped a photo before I could even think about it. I glanced at the pile but didn't see anything else I needed right now.

"How much longer will you be here? Do I need to leave?" I asked

"We're just finishing up," he replied. "Another hour at the most. You're welcome to stay if you keep out of the living room. We've checked the rest of the house and it doesn't look like there's anything for us there."

I headed into my bedroom and sat on the bed. Miraculously my phone still worked, tough little bugger. I started making phone calls. I called Heather, and cried while I told her what happened. I told her not to come. She insisted she'd be here before the day was out. I didn't argue. I called Carlotta, knowing that Doug had probably already called her, and I was right.

"Darla, I'm so sorry! Do you need me to come? I'm at work, but I can be there in a little over an hour. Really. Do you want me there?"

"Not now, Carlotta. I'll need you soon enough, when I figure out what's what. I just wanted to let you know, that's all. Would you make sure Sam knows, too, although Doug probably called him?" And I cried again.

"Don't you worry, girlfriend. We'll get you what you need, and I'll help any way I can. Call me later to let me know what I can do."

"Yeah, okay." I ended the call and then stared at the phone wondering who to call next. Paul, I suppose. I chose his number from my favorites log. He answered on the first ring.

"Darla? Where are you? Are you alright?" he asked.

"I'm at my house. Where are you?" I asked.

"I'm at the station. I took a few hours off but stopped by to find out if they know anything new. I'm talking with Detective Rodriguez right now."

"And do they? Know anything new?" I asked.

"Of course, they're working on the assumption that this was Meurtrier," Paul said.

"What? I thought he was in custody!" I nearly screamed.

"Meurtrier's attorney somehow got him released on bond as part of the agreement, not taking into consideration that Texas was trying to extradite him. I was in town working with Rodriguez when the call came in about the fire. They know where he is but they can't pick him up until they have something new from the forensics crew. You know how these things go. I'll call you as soon as I know anything. In the meantime, try not to worry." He disconnected.

As far as I could tell, between the witness protection program and Allie's handler, Texas and Tennessee state interactions, and the FBI, lines of communication were not exactly open. Yes, I did know how these things go. Slowly. In the meantime, I felt exposed and at risk. Try not to worry, my foot! It occurred to me that I might be putting Jeanette and Wayne at risk too, just by staying with them. I'd get a hotel room tonight.

My caller bag was in the office. I stepped out of the bedroom and looked to see if I could make my way to the office without interfering. The path was clear. Once in the office, I started making more calls. I called until I found a substitute caller for Forsby and Clearton this week at least. Next I sent a text to Carlotta asking her to let the club officers know who their callers would be.

Those calls behind me, it was time to start the insurance ball rolling. I called my insurance agent, one of the best. He offered sympathy first, then said he would be out as soon as possible to look over the damage and see what he could do to help me.

I poked my head out the office door and called "Tom? Do you have a minute?"

Tom appeared.

"Tom, what about the utilities? Are the water and electricity on?" I caught my breath as a thought occurred to me. "What about gas? Surely they cut off the gas, right?" I asked.

"Yes, ma'am. The fire department always cuts off the gas first thing. Thankfully, the fire didn't get to the gas lines or hot water heater. They shut off the other utilities before they left and notified the utility companies. You'll need to contact the utilities company and they'll have to green light it before they turn them back on. They don't bother with cable but you'll want to notify the company to check the connections."

"Thanks," I said.

"Was that all?" he asked.

"Yes. No. Sorry, my brain is working on half-power for now." I told him.

"That's fine, no problem, what else?"

"Tom, I don't remember much after crawling and getting to tile. How did I end up outside?"

"The glass door to your patio. When one of the firemen shined his flashlight in he saw something. He went in to check and found you, pulled you out, ma'am. Oh, he had to jimmy that door, so you might want to get it checked out."

I nodded and he headed back to the office.

I called the utilities next to find out what I needed to do. That handled, I sat back and wondered what to do. It was a little overwhelming. No, it was a lot overwhelming. I was still sitting in the same position when Tom Terrific came to tell me his team was packing up to leave.

"So it's okay for me to clean up everything now?" I asked.

"Right as rain. I talked with Detective Rodriguez and he cleared it."

He hesitated, then added, "I know it's a bit daunting, Ms. King, but in my experience something like this should clean up nicely. Don't try to do it yourself, hire a good restoration company."

With that, he was gone and I was alone. I heard the front door close and then quiet. I took a deep breath and braved the scene in the living room. It looked pretty bad to me. I went back to the bedroom, sat on the bed and cried, again.

Eventually, I searched through my purse and found my keys. At least I could lock up this time. Unlike after the break-in. I threaded my way around the black hole in the living room and into the kitchen. I locked the patio door as best I could and gave it a test jerk. I made a mental note to find out whether I needed to repair or replace it. Probably replace it. The good thing about the patio door was that the fireman was able to see me and get me out. The bad thing was that didn't leave me feeling very secure. I locked the front door as I left. Even with all the windows shattered, being able to lock doors made me feel better. Silly, since the shattered windows provided easy access to anyone. Sighing, I added calling to get the windows repaired to my mental to-do list.

I went back to Jeanette and Wayne's. They wanted to know what was happening. I had a feeling I'd be repeating the story, in whole or in part, many times in the coming weeks. Bless Jeanette, she made me lunch and we talked about everything but my fire over the meal.

Heather showed up late afternoon. I asked her about classes, but she assured me she was doing fine and could miss a week or so. One of her classes was online, so she promised to keep up with it while she was home. I didn't protest too much, since I was happy to have her with me. I didn't want to impose on Jeanette and Wayne, however, and I was still aware that I might be putting them in danger.

Heather's arrival gave me a good excuse to thank them and head for a nearby hotel. Heather and I shared a room, and she caught me up on her life when we got settled in. I left dealing with the house for another day.

Chapter 21

Heather was amazing. I had raised her the best I could, but she had turned out way better than I had any right to hope. She kept me calm and knew just what to do to take care of things. More than I did. When I asked her how she knew what to do, she'd say "I Googled it," or "I just went online, Mom."

I contacted the restoration company and they cleaned up the mess. I arranged to get a dumpster pulled into the driveway to make it easier to ditch the furniture, the CD sculpture, and the carpet from the living room. The restoration company did a great job. The hardware store came with new windows and a new patio door. They were followed by the painters. Heather and I went shopping and picked out new furniture. I only got the basics. This was getting expensive and it wasn't clear when the insurance company would give me a check.

We were in the hotel room looking at carpet samples Tuesday afternoon when she said, "Mom, there's something I need to tell you."

"What? You don't like the beige carpet choice?" I shot back.

"No, really. It's important, I just didn't know how to tell you," she said. Uh-oh. I could tell by her expression and her tone that this was serious. My mind immediately flew to a dozen different options, each scarier than the first.

"Okay. Heather, I want you to be able to tell me anything," I said.

"I want that, too, Mom. But you know it hasn't always been the case," she replied.

"What do you mean?"

"Oh come on, Mom. Do you tell me everything? What about the break-in at your house? What about your romance with Paul? I'm sure there's lots more I don't even know you haven't told me." She was being calm, still I could hear anger seeping into her words.

"You're my child, Heather. I'm your mother. There are some things I can't tell you. I don't want to worry you and, sometimes, I'm just embarrassed to talk with you about things." It sounded reasonable to me.

"I'm not a kid anymore, Mom. We're getting married." I was still on the tangent about telling each other about everything and it took me a moment to change gears.

"What?"

"Married, Mom. Me and Micah. I wanted to tell you earlier, but... Well, anyway, I wanted to tell you," she trailed off.

"How soon, Heather? Have you set a date? Are you sure Micah is the one for you?" Too many questions, I was asking too many questions. I should just be happy for her. I tried again.

"I'm happy for you, Heather. Really, whether I sound like it or not. I wish you would have told me sooner." Nope, that wasn't right either. I sounded like I was scolding her. I tried once more. "I love you, baby. Tell me about it, please." Better, I thought.

And she did. She glowed when she talked about Micah, and I hoped it was the real thing for her. As she talked, I realized again what a wonderful young woman she had grown up to be. And grown up she was. No longer my little girl. I'd have to get used to that, figure out how to relate to her in this new grown-up way.

"So when I was down here a few weeks ago, you know, when Paul was here, I came to go look at wedding dresses. Brandy and Courtney and I went."

She must have read my face, since she immediately followed up with, "But I didn't buy one yet, Mom. I want you to go shopping with me. And not just for your credit card, either!" she ended with a laugh.

"Oh, Heather, I'm so sorry you didn't feel like you could tell me. That I didn't make it easy for you to talk to me, on that trip or any other time. From here on out, can we try to talk to each other about everything? Anything? I will try, too, I promise," I said.

We spent the rest of the afternoon looking at wedding dresses online instead of carpet samples. They hadn't set a date yet. She wanted a simple wedding. I wanted to give her an engagement party. More than anything, I wanted to love her the right way. The way she needed. I resolved to try my best to keep the communication lines open with her.

I didn't hear much from Paul, at least not much constructive. He was thoroughly entrenched in the case now, and didn't have time for much else. He and the police department and fire department were all sure the Molotov cocktail was a warning from Meurtrier. It wouldn't make sense for him to try to burn down my house if he believed the money was hidden there. The theory was he knew he had searched the living room during the break-in so he strategically started the fire in that room.

I wasn't so sure. I still believed Allie was the driving force, and capable of anything. Paul wasn't clear about whether Allie was working with Meurtrier, and no one knew where either of them were hiding.

By Wednesday night, with mostly everything cleaned up, Heather asked why we were still at the hotel. Jeanette had asked as well. In the spirit of being open and honest, I explained to Heather that with Meurtrier and Allie still free, I was a bit afraid of the next warning. I talked to Detective Rodriguez and Officer Johnson, but the best the Isquith police could do was arrange for a drive-by on a regular basis. We decided it was time, fear or not, and checked out of the hotel Thursday morning.

Also on Thursday morning, Doug called. It was good to hear from him. After the usual chit chat and an update on the house, he got around to the purpose of his call.

"I thought you might want to come see the camp."

"Oh Doug, I can't. There's so much to do after the fire," I replied.

"I thought you might want to come see me and the camp," he repeated.

I assumed he hadn't heard me. "I'm sorry, Doug. I can't. Heather and I are trying to get the house back in shape."

"I thought you might want to come see me," he said. Then I got it. The emphasis on 'me' did the trick.

"Oh. Yes, I would. Let me check with Heather and I'll call you back."

Okay, my next hurdle as a communicating mom. I tried to explain to Heather the complex relationship between Doug and me. She knew Doug from the time she'd lived here and liked him a lot. Although she knew we dated for a while, she didn't realize the role Doug had played in the investigation of her dad's death or how much I had depended on Doug when we moved to Isquith. I explained it all as clearly as I could, given that I didn't really understand it that well myself.

"Mom, you don't need to worry about the house. I'll take care of that for the rest of today," she offered. "But what about your friend Paul?"

She was sharp, that daughter of mine. Yes, what about my friend Paul?

"Yeah, that's a tough one," I answered. "Got any ideas?" She didn't.

I called Doug back and asked him if I could come on out in an hour or so. It would take about an hour after that to reach his ranch.

"That sounds good," he said. "I'll have some lunch ready for you."

On the way out to his place, my mind tossed with what I would say. I went over the night of the fire, and how I knew I wanted to call him even though Paul was already there. I remembered how safe I felt in his arms and that I never wanted to leave them. What on earth was I going to tell him?

I'd been to his house lots of times, but this time I was nervous. He has a spread of about 500 acres, and he's fenced off a small yard area around his house. The rest is fenced into acreage for horses and cattle to graze, for growing hay, and now for camp activities.

I saw a couple of his riding horses saddled and tethered at the fence and looked down at my tennis shoes. I hadn't dressed for riding, but these should work. I walked across his wide front porch and knocked on the screen door.

"Come on in." I heard Doug's voice coming from the kitchen and let myself in. He met me in the living room and gave me a quick hug.

"I fixed King Ranch chicken. Work for you?" he asked.

"Works great for me. I love King Ranch," I said.

"Good. I've got it all ready. I thought we'd eat and then go for a ride and I'll show you the plans for expanding the therapy camp," he said.

He had the table already set, and we visited while we ate. King Ranch chicken, salad, and garlic bread. A feast in my opinion. We talked mainly about the camp, a little about how Nationals went, and a few other things. I helped him clean up and we headed out to the horses.

It had been a while since I'd been in a saddle. It took me a couple of tries to get up, but I made it not too ungracefully. After convincing Star I was in charge, she settled into a smooth walk and I rode by Doug's side toward the barn and beyond.

"Right now we use the round pen," he explained, motioning to the heavy metal panels set into the ground in a circle near the barn. "I want to put up some bleachers around the outside so parents can watch and the kids who are waiting can sit down."

"What do you do exactly during equine therapy?" I asked.

"Mainly, just riding the horses helps some kids. For others it's learning to take charge of something. Or it's learning responsibility for brushing and feeding the horse after the session. Lots of ways it helps. I know a little about it, but I don't do the therapy. We have qualified people for that. I'm just making my ranch and horses available," he said.

We rode on, mostly in silence, appreciating the day and the scenery. He pulled his horse to a stop at the top of a small hill. He pointed down to the fence below.

"That's the end of my property down there," he said. "Between this hill and that fence, I want to build a facility to house the camp. Like a rodeo coliseum. Part of it will be floored, part of it dirt. That way the weather won't get in the way of camp activities, and the facility will be versatile for lots of different kinds of activities." I could hear the enthusiasm in his voice. "Even a square dance, maybe," he said with a grin.

"Doug, that sounds wonderful. You've really gone through a lot to get this thing going, haven't you?" I asked.

"Yeah. I guess it's been about three years since I first got the idea. A friend of mine had a kid who went to equine therapy and it did him a world of good. But it was really expensive. I decided I wanted that type of experience to be affordable to lots more kids. That's why I set this up as a nonprofit. Although I met a lot of resistance from the community at first, now most everyone has embraced it."

"It's a truly worthwhile endeavor, and you should be proud. Sounds like you have a lot of ideas for expanding it," I said.

"Thanks." He turned in the saddle to face me. "But you know showing you the camp is only one reason for this ride, don't you. I told you at your house, we need to talk."

"I know. You start," I said.

"Okay, I will. I just want you to be happy, Darla. If it takes Paul to do that, then fine. But somehow I don't think he's making you happy. Am I wrong? You called me even though he was already at your house the night of the fire. What was that all about, Darla?"

"I don't know myself, Doug. I just knew I wanted to hear your voice and have you there. I'm sorry if it caused you any problems," I said.

"No problems for me. I was happy to be there. I would love to be there for you all the time, Darla. You know that. You're the one that said 'just friends.' Remember?" He paused a minute and added, "Do you mind if we get down from the horses to be more comfortable?"

"Sure," I agreed. We both dismounted and dropped the reins down. Doug opened his saddlebags, pulled out two bottles of water, and handed me one. He motioned to a nearby oak and we aimed for the shade. When we were settled on the ground, he looked at me.

"Your turn," he said.

"I'm struggling, Doug. With our history together, you know that. You know I love your company. What about you and Cassie? That makes a difference, too," I said.

"Cassie and I aren't romantic. She's my camp director. We tried dating for a while and I introduced her to square dancing. But we just didn't click in that department, so now we're just colleagues and dance partners."

With a glint in his eye, he said, "Lucky for me, I seem to be able to remain friends with my exes, so it's no problem working together."

Well, that was a surprise. I sure thought they were a couple.

"Darla," he continued. "You've got to let me know. You've got to make up your mind. If it's Paul you want, or just not me you want, I'll respect that. It didn't feel like that the other night though."

"It's complicated," I said. He rolled his eyes. "Yes, I know, everyone says that. Romance is complicated across the board, I guess," I hurried on. "Paul's a great guy, but I find myself getting aggravated with him too often. That's not a good sign if it crops up even in the beginning of a relationship. With you, I feel good. I feel safe. I feel … loved."

"I don't want good. I don't want safe, Darla. At least not only those. I want the whole package. Am I off base here?"

"No, you're not. I need to finalize things with Paul, though, and this isn't a good time. He's right in the middle of working the case of Jake's murder."

"There's never a good time to break off with someone, Darla. You know that. On the other hand, it's not right to keep it going if you don't feel it."

I knew he was right. "Don't write me off, Doug. Give me a week and I'll get back with you. I do want us to give it another try."

"I'll never write you off as a friend, Darla. Anything else, you're holding the upper hand," he said. "Can we hug it out before we head back to the house?"

And we did. We stood up and I brushed the grass off my jeans. We stepped into an embrace, awkward at first, then comfortable. Just as it was moving from comfortable to something else for me, he pulled away.

"Let's get these horses back to the barn. They're due for riding this afternoon at the camp," he said.

After the ride, I went home. I was worried about Heather. I didn't like that she was there alone. We had a quiet dinner. Heather had stayed most of the week and it felt like we had made a lot of progress in improved communication. But all good things must come to an end and she needed to return to Austin and her studies. She would head back the next morning. We checked all the doors and windows before turning in.

Chapter 22

My eyes were teary as I watched Heather drive away Friday morning. I waved to her and set about cleaning up our breakfast dishes. The carpet was getting laid today and the furniture would arrive for the living room. We'd picked out a simple couch, two chairs, and some occasional tables. The coffee table and entertainment center had cleaned up well enough. Jeanette and Wayne came by but we had little chance to talk with all the activity going on.

"Darla, you've done a great job redecorating," Jeanette yelled over the noise, glancing around. "At least, as much as I can tell. When will they get it all in place?"

"They tell me today." I looked around too, doubtful. "I hope it all comes together."

"Don't worry, it will," Jeanette reassured me.

Wayne chimed in, "And if it doesn't, you've got a willing handyman just next door!"

"I've already called on that handyman too often lately," I laughed in response. "I have to admit he's a great one!"

"We'll let you get back to taking care of things. Call us if you need us," Jeanette said, and hugged me goodbye. I regretted seeing them leave, and was surprised how quickly the morning went by. Sure enough, by lunchtime the carpet was down and the furniture in place. I still had to take all the plastic off, but my living room looked livable again.

Restless, I checked the flowerbeds and watered. Everything looked dry. I remembered I had some garden soil in the small shed on the patio and decided to take some time to work in the front yard. I certainly needed the distraction. I walked around the side of the house to the patio. Sure enough, in the shed I could see the bag of garden soil behind the large pots I had stuck there. Unfortunately, that meant taking the pots out first. As I moved the first one, something fell on my foot. I jumped, and heard skittering across the floor.

I stepped out of the shed to let light in through the doorway. As I did, I stepped on a rock that pushed down into the dry ground. A shaft of light fell into the shed and something sparkled. Several somethings sparkled. Lots of somethings sparkled. Confused, I knelt down to see what had scattered across the shed floor and out into the dirt.

At first I thought a vase had broken and shattered. I didn't remember having any colored glass vases out here. I reached out and picked up one of the sparkling objects and put it in the palm of my hand to examine. It looked for all the world like an emerald. I picked up another. A diamond? Another. A red stone. The light slowly transferred from the stones to my brain. These were jewels. A whole slew of jewels.

After looking over my shoulder to make sure I was alone, I picked up one of my flower pots, checking that it was one without a drain hole in the bottom. Then, one by one, I picked up all the stones I could find and set them in the pot. With just the meager lighting from outside, I couldn't be sure what was what and picked up some rocks along with jewels. Eventually, I worked my way back to the item that had fallen on my foot in the first place. It was a small newspaper-wrapped packet that had burst open. It still held a good number of stones and I put the whole thing in the flower pot.

Looking around to make sure I hadn't missed anything or anyone, I closed the door to the shed and carried the pot into the house. I set it on the counter. Moved it to the table. Moved it inside the cabinet under the sink. Still wasn't happy with it there.

Paranoid, I locked all the doors and checked the windows. All secure. I opened the cabinet and stared into the pot. The jewels glowed like little sparkly peas. Peas in a pot. Peas in a pod. Wait! Frozen peas! It's where people sometimes hide money, in the freezer! I'd replaced my frozen food after the break-in, and one thing I bought was frozen peas.

I walked deliberately to the freezer and pulled out the bag of peas. I took it to the sink and carefully sliced it open. Peas skittered into the sink I washed them down the disposal. I rinsed the sink and put in the stopper. Gently I poured all the jewels from the pot into the pea bag. I sealed it with clear tape and put it in the freezer under a roast.

I set the empty pot by the patio door, went to my new couch, and sat.

Both Meurtrier and Allie were right. Jake had left his stash with me. I just didn't know it. A part of the story Meurtrier had given Paul still didn't make sense, but it was becoming clearer what the true version was. After a few minutes, I texted Paul and asked him to call me as soon as he could. I typed "URGENT" in all caps. And then I waited. I stepped into the closet to take the call in case the house was bugged. I knew it was unlikely, still, after all that had happened I wasn't taking any chances. Besides, you're not paranoid if people are really after you.

Paul sounded annoyed at my text until I whispered that I had found something he would want to see. Something hidden, I said. He said he was on his way. About an hour later, the doorbell rang. Through the peephole I could see Officer Johnson.

I opened the door and she explained, "Agent Harbinville asked me to meet him here. Is he here yet?"

"He should be here any minute. Did he tell you why he wanted you to meet him?"

"He just called the station. Detective Rodriguez is in a meeting, so he asked for me. Said he had some information on the murder and to meet him here. I'm not sure what he could add. The murderer is finally supposed to be extradited from Tennessee sometime today."

I invited her in. With my polite upbringing, I offered her iced tea or water and we sat in the living room with little conversation. She commented on some of the pictures in the room of square dancers and I mechanically explained what a square dance caller did.

Paul finally arrived. He barely gave me a kiss before he directed his attention to Officer Johnson. "Officer Johnson, I asked you to meet me here so you can be a witness. Darla found something that was hidden, and I'm thinking she meant by Jake, is that right, Darla?" I nodded. "Probably the reason Meurtrier killed him," he continued.

He pulled out his notebook and looked at me to explain. I recounted what I'd found, which I was happy to see took them by surprise too. I explained how I'd found it, brought it in, and hid it again. Paul stopped writing and looked about to explode. "You moved it? You destroyed the chain of evidence!"

"I couldn't very well leave it scattered across the patio, could I? Did you expect me to sit on it like a brood hen? I had to do something with it!" I defended myself. I heard Officer Johnson stifle a laugh.

"Okay, okay," she said "Agent Harbinville, Ms. King, that's all water under the bridge. Where is it now?" Officer Johnson moved between us.

I looked to Paul and he nodded slightly. I told them where it was and turned to get it. Paul and Officer Johnson both stopped me at one time.

"I'll get it," Paul said.

"We'll get it together," Officer Johnson countered. "Nobody move. I mean it." She moved faster than I'd seen her move before, out the front door and quickly reappeared with an evidence bag in hand.

Together we trooped to the kitchen. We verified the condition of the bag while Paul rolled his eyes about a frozen pea bag. Officer Johnson slipped it into the evidence bag like it was a normal occurrence. She clicked a picture of it and all of us signed off that Paul was taking possession of it in his role as representing the FBI for the Schwindle case. Officer Johnson called in for a forensic team to come check the patio area and verified that Paul would remain here until they came. Paul said he would stay, made several calls, and Officer Johnson left. It didn't take the forensic team long to arrive. When they did, Paul told me he'd be back in a few hours and took off.

This was the same forensics team that had come out after the fire. I couldn't remember Tom's last name, since 'Tom Terrific' had stuck in my brain. So I greeted him by his first name.

"Hello, Tom. Feel like you've been here before?" I asked.

He smiled. "Yes, but it looks a lot better than it did last time," he said.

"I'll show you where I found ..." I hesitated. He knew about the jewels, right? Of course he did, he had to know to do his job. My brain was working slowly today "...where I found the jewels. It's out back," I finished up. We walked out the patio door together and over to the potting shed.

"If you need me, I'll be inside," I said.

If I was tired before, I was exhausted now. I was also very conflicted about Paul saying he was coming back. He just assumed I wanted him to. That didn't sit well. On the other hand, even in Meurtrier is under arrest like Officer Johnson thought, what about Allie? And tonight I would be alone if Paul didn't come back. If he did, it might be a good opportunity to bring up our relationship and let him know it wasn't enough for me.

I pulled up the local and state news on the computer to see if there was any announcement about Meurtrier. I couldn't find anything. Frustrating not knowing, I tried a few search engines and gave up. I shifted gears and pulled up my square dance files. This was more fun and I hadn't updated or played around with new songs since the caller convention.

"Ms. King?" Tom Terrific's voice cut through my concentration.

"Yes?" I responded.

"We've finished up outside. But please leave the tape and markers in place for now. An officer will give you the go-ahead to remove them later."

I thanked him and walked to the front door to watch them leave. Back in the office, I worked on calls and songs as a distraction until my growling stomach let me know it was past time for dinner. It had been over four hours and no word from Paul. I pulled dinner together and got ready to eat, humming and feeling pretty good in spite of the past few weeks and my crazy life. Surely all the upheaval was coming to an end now, at least with my neighbors if not with my personal life.

I had no sooner sat down to eat when I heard something from the front of the house. After only a moment's hesitation, I grabbed a butcher knife and walked toward the front door. I saw a flash of movement out one of the new windows in the living room, and dropped to the floor behind the sofa. I peeked around and caught a definite movement going past the other window. I was glad I'd spent the extra money on safety and eco-friendly glass and screens.

I crawled over to pull my phone out of my purse and called 911. I told the dispatcher I thought someone was prowling in my yard and she had me stay on the line. It wasn't long before I heard a lot of noise and the dispatcher said, "Officers have arrived on the scene. Stay where you are until they give the all clear." I would have thanked her, if she hadn't already disconnected.

A few minutes later the doorbell chimed. I yelled, "Who's there?"

"Officer Johnson, Ms. King."

I went to the door and opened it. She stood there along with another officer, who held Allie's elbow. Allie didn't look too happy, but I have to give her credit. She was still dressed in high fashion. Only her haughty, angry expression marred the picture.

"Ms. King, we found this person in your yard. I'm afraid you'll need to replace one of your screens," Officer Johnson offered as she showed me wire clippers.

Oh, my, it was time to think about a security system or maybe reconsider the gun ownership option. Allie squirmed and the other officer tightened his grip. For sure, if looks could kill, I'd have been dead.

"You, you have it don't you? Where is it? That money is mine!" Allie hissed.

"I told you Allie, I never saw Jake except that once at your house. And I don't have your money."

"Ms. King, we will need to complete a report..."

Paul's car screeched to a halt and he jumped out of the car. "Darla, are you alright?"

I nodded and he moved as if to take over.

"Agent Harbinville, we have this under control here. I was just explaining to Ms. King that she will need to complete a report, but for now we're taking this prowler down to the station. She's under arrest for trespass and destruction of property. If you or anyone else wants to add to those charges, you know where she'll be."

With that Officer Johnson and her associate dragged Allie to the waiting cruiser. I almost laughed at Paul's expression of surprise. I don't think anyone had ever run over him like that. Between his federal badge and his good looks, he was quite used to getting his way.

He recovered quickly and I invited him in. He wanted to know what had happened. I told him I'd trade my information for his. Grudgingly, he filled me in on his busy afternoon. Meurtrier had been arrested and extradited to Texas. He was in a high-security facility awaiting trial on several charges at state and federal levels. Once Schwindle was convicted, which was all but guaranteed now, the money in the Schwindle accounts would be recovered and returned to the people who could be verified. Not all the money had been recovered, but they were working on it. The value of the jewels would be added to it.

"And, Darla, at some point, you will be receiving a check for $1000 for your part in recovery of the money. A reward for your troubles. Don't go spending it all in one place!" he teased.

I knew exactly what I would do with the reward. It would help considerably with the new facility at Doug's camp.

He walked into the kitchen and spotted my dinner, not yet eaten. "Shall we go out and get some dinner?"

"Yeah, that would be good." My dinner was ice cold and not that appetizing any more. Dinner would give me a good opportunity to discuss our relationship, too. I freshened up and tried to plan what I would say when I had the chance. I needed – no, wanted – more emotional commitment, to matter more than his cases. I didn't and that just wasn't good enough for me.

Back in the living room, Paul was checking out the furniture and the new pictures on the wall. "You and Heather did a nice job in here. It looks good."

"Thanks! We had trouble deciding on the colors, but I wanted something a little different." Pointing to an empty spot on the wall, I added, "I found a copy of Heather's graduation picture and I'm having it enlarged and framed to go there."

He nodded and pulled me into his arms. "You've been through a lot these past few weeks. At least there was a silver lining in the time you spent with Heather, the redo of the living room, and now the reward." I would just have soon done without getting that silver lining this way, but I didn't say anything.

He added, "Just one more thing about the case. I'll need to go down to the station tonight to find out what Allie has to say, and make some calls. Until then, I'm all yours."

I stepped out of his embrace and we left for dinner. He didn't ask but I'd already known we were going to the local steak house. I also knew exactly what he would order, and if I ordered something different from my "usual" that he would question my choice. I must have sighed out loud because he looked at me with his eyebrows raised in question.

"Just thinking." I smiled and, as we sat down and he proceeded to order exactly what I expected, I smiled again. If only I could appreciate his excellent qualities without resenting others. As we drank our after dinner coffees, I decided it was time to broach the subject.

"Paul, I think we need to talk about our relationship."

He reached over for my hand and responded, "Darla, didn't we talk about this already? If I overstep it's only that I want you to be safe and you keep ending up in these dangerous situations."

"Paul, I get that. I really do. And I understand that you need to be in charge and involved in any mystery or case I stumble on, because that's who you are. It's the take charge attitude and your strength that attracted me to you. Besides your sexy good looks, of course!" I smiled to temper the sting of what I was about to say. "The problem is it is also one part of why I don't think this is going to work." There, I'd said it.

"What? What do you mean? I don't see a problem."

"When things are going well, it seems like it will work okay. You can be funny and we enjoy some of the same things. It's just…"

"…that I don't square dance?"

"No, Paul, that's not all of it." Geesh, he focused on details! "I mean, yes, for a long-term relationship, that would be part of the issue. Because you don't square dance, I don't get to dance even when I have the chance. For square dance purposes, I'm solo. More important, square dancing is a big part of my life and it feels to me that you're discounting part of my life by not participating in it in some way. But square dancing isn't the whole thing. When a crisis occurs, when things are falling apart, I want someone I can lean on, whose attention is on me, not the crisis. For you, the crisis is more important."

He let go of my hand and leaned back. "I don't know what to say. I do care about you, Darla. I thought you cared about me. And yes, I do get focused on a case instead of the people. It is an occupational hazard and safeguard. I think it's been a real stressful few weeks. We can let it go for a few weeks and then see how you feel." He took my hand again and suggested, "Let's see how you feel after life gets back to normal."

I smiled and decided that was a start. I didn't have to say it all right now, did I? I took the coward's way out. I'd figure out what was happening with Doug, and in the meantime I had an engagement party to plan.

Chapter 23

Carlotta had told me several times lately that she needed some face time with me. I was glad, because I needed a best friend's advice. I'd tried to break it off with Paul and taken the easy road instead. After searching inward a little more, I knew where my heart wanted to go. And my heart was finally ready to take the trip. Maybe I was growing up as much as Heather was.

Saturday morning, I called up Carlotta.

"Carlotta, it's Darla. Wondering if you have some time to get together this weekend. For a change, I don't have any calling obligations. Want to come over to my house and spend tonight with me? I'll even cook dinner!"

"Great timing, Darla. I was just wondering what I was going to do for fun on a Saturday. Couldn't find a dance going on anywhere. Something up?" she asked.

"No. Well, yes. Um, you know, I just need some advice from my best friend," I stammered out. I didn't want to get into it over the phone.

"I've always got free advice. Usually worth what you pay for it, though, so watch out! How about 2 or 3 this afternoon?"

"Perfect. See you then, Carlotta."

I figured a slow-cooker meal would be the easiest. I sliced up a head of cabbage, stacked on several pork chops, and poured a can of diced tomatoes over it all. Done. That was easy. When we got ready to eat, I'd just set out some carrot and celery sticks with dressing, and bread to go with everything.

I took a few minutes to change the sheets in my guest room and straighten the house. For the first time in a good while I found I had time on my hands. Free time, what was that?

The only times I'd seen Wayne and Jeanette lately were when I was in crisis, so I decided to use my free time to have a non-emergency visit with them and take the first installment of their thank you gift. Getting the gift card at the restaurant took longer than I thought. By the time I got home and picked a few flowers and walked next door, time was flying. So much for free time. Wayne and Jeanette seemed glad to see me and we got about 30 minutes of visiting in before I told them I had company coming. I headed back to my house.

I was still a little frightened of another attack so I continually scanned my surroundings on the short walk to and from their house. Nothing seemed out of the ordinary, and I was plenty ready for ordinary. The house smelled great when I walked in. I checked the pork chops and the clock. My phone rang just as I heard Carlotta's car pull up in my drive. Glancing at the screen, I saw it was Paul.

"Hi, Paul. Where are you this weekend?" I greeted him. With phone at my ear, I opened the door to Carlotta. We waved silently and I motioned her inside. She pointed to her car and made an about-face.

"I'm in Dallas right now," Paul said. Lord, I hoped he doesn't want to come see me. Not this weekend, I thought.

He went on, "I thought I'd have a little time off this weekend and you could come up. Turns out I have to head to Virginia on a late flight tonight instead," he explained. Saved by his work, the very thing that was torpedoing my relationship with him. Isn't life funny.

"Not the Carstairs case, is it?" I asked.

"No, another one. Sorry I can't see you, though. What's on your agenda?" he asked.

"Carlotta and I are finally gonna get some girl-talk time together," I told him. "She's just arrived, as a matter of fact."

"Glad you won't be alone or bored either. We'll talk soon, Darla. Stay safe, I mean it!" he said.

We closed out the call, and I realized we seldom ended our calls with 'I love you.' It was the first time I'd noticed it. I guess a little distance gave me some perspective.

Carlotta returned rolling her suitcase behind her. After a quick hug, she headed toward the guest room.

"So who was on the phone?" she asked.

I followed in her wake. "Paul. Just checking in," I told her.

She stopped and faced me. "Well, that was a pretty quick conversation for 'significant others.' Unless you'd been talking a long time before I got here."

"No, he called just as you pulled up. We don't usually have long conversations," I answered

"That's not good," she said. Laughing, she added, "You did say you wanted my opinions, right? There's the first one. More to come!"

"You'll have opinions, all right. When I tell you what I want to talk about," I said. I held up my pinky finger and crooked it, as any preteen girl knows how to do. "But first, you've got to Secret Swear. Really, you can't tell anyone what we talk about." Yes, I felt like an idiot. Still I needed reassurance.

"Holy moly, this must be good!" She hooked her pinky through mine and gave it a tug. "Secret Swear! Secret Swear! Now spill it."

"Doug and I have decided to give our relationship another try," I told her.

"I knew it! I knew it! You guys are great together!" As usual, Carlotta radiated energy. She threw her purse and keys on the bed and grabbed me in a bearhug. She bounced up and down, and if I'd been any lighter she would have lifted me off the floor. All motion stopped abruptly. Keeping her hands on my shoulders, she took a step back.

"Ooh. How did Mr. FBI take it?" she asked.

I broke eye contact and looked at my feet. "I haven't told him. I mean, I tried to tell him. You know Paul. He's not the best listener. I told him our relationship wasn't working, but I didn't mention Doug's name. He said we should just get through the past few rough weeks, and I didn't contradict him. I botched it."

I looked up again and continued, "That's why you're here, Carlotta. I need some help."

"I'm not going to break up with him for you, girlfriend. But I can sure offer some support to shore you up. Come on."

She hooked her elbow through mine and marched us into the living room. We plopped down together on the new couch. She looked around the room appreciatively.

"I like what you've done with the place," she said. She sniffed the air like a prairie dog. "I don't smell any smoke. How'd that happen?"

"The restoration company was great. They have some magic concoction that neutralizes the odor." I sighed. "Of course, it doesn't hurt that every darn thing in here is new from the carpet up. I can still smell a whiff of smoke every now and then when I walk into my closet, but that's it. Carlotta, you can't imagine how wonderfully helpful Heather was in this whole process."

"Heather! Now there's something else we need to talk about. I want to hear all about the engagement party. And her fiancé. And her. Whew, you've got romance in the air from all corners, don't you?"

"I'm overwhelmed by it all. But you know, somehow I feel good at the same time. Oh, it's hard to explain."

"I gotcha, girlfriend." She eyed me critically. "But it's not fair to Mr. Hunk not to tell him the score. You can't keep him hoping when you know there's no hope."

"That's not the first time I've heard that," I admitted. "It's true. I just don't know how to talk about it with him. That's where I need your advice," I said.

"Advice I can do. Let's dish!"

And dish we did. With words, with pork chops and cabbage, a few times with tears. It was a long and therapeutic evening. About 2:00 a.m. we called it a night.

After Carlotta left Sunday morning I felt restless, thinking about how I would talk to Paul. On one hand, I needed to do it soon. He deserved that. On the other hand, I couldn't do it in a text message or phone call and we had no plans to meet. On one hand, we'd always been straight with each other so I didn't want to beat around the bush. On the other hand, something like this needed to be said gently. On one hand…. It went on all morning.

I roused myself and made a cup of soup. After that I wandered around cyberspace for a bit without finding anything of interest. I decided I needed a nap after my late night talking to Carlotta, and settled my mind into welcome oblivion. The shadows stretched across the yard when I finally woke up. I called Heather to see how she was doing and she was walking on air, naturally. I phoned my sister Julia. Heather had already told her about the engagement, so we chatted about that briefly. She'd developed a new hobby, scrapbooking, and we spent most of the conversation talking about it, and her, as usual. We seldom talked about anything else, but that was fine with me. It made me feel connected. I went to bed hoping my nap wouldn't keep me from sleeping and it didn't.

Monday I came out of my fog. I realized I hadn't done laundry in a week. Dirty clothes were piled up in the utility room and I added the sheets from the guest room to the pile. I threw a load into the washing machine and went to make a cup of coffee. While sipping, I planned out all the errands I needed to run.

I pitched another load of clothes into the washer and stuffed the wet ones into my dryer. I debated the wisdom of leaving both machines going while I ran errands and decided to throw caution to the wind. Grabbing my keys, purse, and shoes I headed into town. Sure enough, all was well when I returned and I managed to get almost half the clothes washed and dried before I fizzled out. Laundry and errands taken care of, I worked a bit in the garden. It was a productive day despite still worrying about breaking up with Paul.

Tuesday I was restless. I was still mulling over how to end my relationship with Paul, and now I had another stressor. I'd be seeing Doug at Clearton tonight. And Carlotta. I didn't want to have to explain anything to Doug yet, and I hoped Carlotta hadn't said anything about our talk. I targeted my anxiety toward my calling routine for the night. I wanted to have enough regular songs on tap that I could carry on if I got flustered. At the same time, the Clearton group thrived on new songs and fresh choreography. After some thought, I arrived at a lineup that satisfied me.

I checked the contents of my overnight bag and returned it to the car. I rifled through my closet and eventually found a long skirt and t-shirt that felt right. I still had several hours before I needed to go to Clearton. To fill the time, I gave Heather a buzz. She answered on the first ring.

"Mom! Is everything okay?" she asked.

"Fine, honey. How are you doing?" I asked her.

"Everything's okay here, Mom. Just hectic at the end of semester. You never call me this often, are you sure you're okay?"

"Absolutely. I've just been thinking of you a lot, Heather. This is an exciting point in your life. We need to talk about your engagement party," I told her.

"Yeah, we do. If everything's all right with you for now, I need to run. I'm on my way to class. Love you, Mom."

"Love you too, honey. I'm proud of you." I think she heard the last sentence before she hung up, but I couldn't be sure.

I picked up and put down my phone twice after talking to Heather. The third time I picked it up, I dialed Doug's number before I could change my mind.

"Hey Doug," I said.

"Hey yourself. Everything okay?" he asked.

"Fine. I was just thinking about tonight."

"Me too. Can't wait to see you," he said. A slight pause then, "What's our status?"

"Doug, I haven't talked to Paul yet . . ." I started out.

"Darla!"

"I haven't talked to Paul YET. He deserves better than a breakup over the phone, Doug. You know that. I plan to see him this weekend."

"Where?"

"I haven't decided yet. Probably Dallas."

"I'll come with you."

Yeah, that would be great, wouldn't it? I couldn't even begin to visualize that meeting.

"No, Doug. I have to do this myself," I said.

"I know you do. I just don't like it," he responded.

"I'm not looking all that forward to it myself," I shot back. I softened my tone and added, "I just wanted to touch base with you before tonight."

"I'm still looking forward to seeing you," he said.

"Me too. Tell me what's happening out at your place," I said.

We talked almost an hour. When we disconnected, I felt better. Except when I thought about calling Paul. Picking up the phone again, I tapped his name. He answered on the third ring. I asked him about his weekend plans. He said he thought he'd be in Dallas.

"We talked about me coming up to see you," I said. "Last weekend didn't work out, but how about this weekend? I really like the Fort Worth Botanic Gardens and I haven't been there in a long time. Want to meet there for a walk Friday?"

I held my breath. I'd churned over multiple locations for our talk. Friday afternoon at the gardens shouldn't be too crowded, and it was a calming spot for the discussion I had in mind. I didn't want to talk over a meal, since it led to all sort of complications. When do you bring up the topic, what if you end the relationship in the middle of the meal, who gets left with the tab? I didn't want to have this talk at his apartment either. This way was cleaner, easier.

"Hold on, let me check. Yes I can do that, Darla. Great idea. What time?" he asked.

"How about I call you when I'm getting close? Probably about 3 or so," I said.

"Sounds good. Be careful, Darla. See you Friday."

That evening, Sam was on the docket for setup duty at Clearton. He was there when I arrived and we chatted while I set up my system. As far as I could tell, Carlotta had kept her Secret Swear. She arrived shortly with Nick in tow.

"Hey, girlfriend! I'm always happy when you're calling for us," she greeted me.

"Which is almost every Tuesday, so I'm happy you're happy," I retorted. "Nick, glad to see you could make it. How'd you get time off in the middle of the week?" Nick was from the Dallas area and seldom made it to one of the regular Clearton club dances.

"On my way down to Houston," he said. Looking at Carlotta, he added, "I arranged it specially so I could dance with my girl here."

Doug arrived next, followed closely by a clump of other dancers. He headed toward me, stopping to greet folks along the way. He gave me a square dancer's hug, holding it a little longer than the generic version. No one noticed a thing. Even Sam who usually had the perception of a psychic. Well, at least he didn't let on if he noticed.

Cassie came in wearing jeans and a t-shirt. Tonight wasn't a special dance, just a club night, so outfits ran the gamut. Carlotta as usual wore a short skirt with a full petticoat. Tonight's version was a red and white gingham skirt with a white blouse and red petticoat. Other women wore long skirts, short skirts, jeans, or whatever. Men had it easy. A pair of jeans and a long-sleeved shirt and they were good to go.

"Welcome! Ready to dance?" I called out. The dance got underway. We had a good-sized crowd and it looked like they all enjoyed the evening.

As I was packing to leave, Carlotta came up to me. "Hey, since Nick's in town we're making a night of it. Want to join us at Clearton Café for a bite to eat?"

"You know I love the café," I said. "I'm planning to drive back, though, so I can't stay long."

"Oh?" I could hear the surprise in Carlotta's voice. I think she assumed I'd be staying over at Doug's but I didn't feel right about that until I had my talk with Paul. Uh-oh. What if Doug assumed the same thing? Boy, this romance thing was complicated.

"Yeah, I'll meet you at the café when I leave here. Y'all go ahead," I replied.

Doug was still saying goodbyes to the dancers, and I dawdled over my packing. It didn't take long with just my computer and small speakers but I stretched the time as long as I could. When the last dancer left, he turned to look at me.

"Did Carlotta tell you we were heading to the café?" he asked.

"Yes, I told her I'd meet them there. You going?" I asked.

"Unless you have better things in mind," he teased.

"Doug, I can't stay long. I need to drive home tonight." I didn't offer an explanation.

"I'll take whatever time I can get with you for now, Darla. Later, we may have to renegotiate. I'm a patient man, so do what you need to do," he said.

I did what I needed to do, not what I wanted to do, and slept in my own bed that night.

Chapter 24

Paul and I talked several times during the rest of the week, and I steered the conversations to neutral topics as best I could. With Paul, that wasn't hard. I left for Fort Worth a little before noon Friday. All the way up, I rehearsed how I hoped the conversation would go. Somewhere about Hillsboro, I called to let Paul know I was close. I recommended we meet at the greenhouse near the entrance to the gardens.

He was waiting when I got there, wearing khaki pants and a pullover knit shirt. Very different from his usual business attire, and he looked good. He was still the Harbinville Hunk, handsome and in excellent shape. Despite that, I knew I wanted a relationship with Doug so seeing Paul didn't flip my switches as it usually did. He gave me a quick kiss hello and asked how things were going.

"Busy," I replied. "Have you heard anything more about the Carstairs?"

"Not much. Meurtrier is in custody here in Texas, thanks to both your fire and Jake's murder. We used the fire as additional leverage after his deal to extradite him. Allie's still in custody on the financial end. Seems to be coming together."

"Well then, let's take the day to forget about the case. Today's a day to focus on us. Let's walk over to the Japanese Gardens. I love them," I said.

We took off toward the back acreage and I could see the Japanese Gardens ahead. I didn't get here often enough, but when I did the gardens calmed me. We were soon surrounded by beautifully sculptured shrubs, winding gravel walks, river birch and red pine trees, and blooming plants everywhere. Just off to the left was the tea house with its Zen garden. As we rounded a curve in the path, I saw a vending box holding food for the Koi fish.

"I love feeding the Koi," I said. I put a quarter in the machine and it dispensed a small handful of pellets. I tossed one into the water and that was all it took. Quickly the water at my feet was teeming with brightly colored bodies with gaping mouths hoping for a handout. I threw a few pellets out farther in the water to encourage them to swim out and show off their different patterns and colors, but most of them chose to stay at my feet. Some even flapped their way out of the water on the backs of their companions. I dropped a few pellets directly down and tossed the rest into the pond, brushing my hands against each other to get off the last few grains of food.

"I have to admit, I've never fed Koi. Enthusiastic little creatures, aren't they?" Paul said.

"Yes, and so beautiful. Nature never ceases to amaze me," I answered.

It was time. "Paul, let's have a seat on the bench in the shade. There's something I need to tell you," I said.

We sat, and Paul draped his arm around my shoulders. "Shoot. What's up?" he asked.

"Not long ago, I told you our relationship wasn't working for me…" I began.

"Yes, and we agreed we'd give it some time to get over the bad weeks you've had," he said.

"You're right. I agreed, and I shouldn't have. I was wrong to agree when I knew what I was trying to do was tell you I couldn't give it any more time. That's what I'm telling you now." I said it quietly, proud of myself for saying it at all.

"So that's it for us? You're pretty matter-of-fact about this whole thing. It seems to me we're getting along great. Don't I get a say?"

"For a relationship to succeed, Paul, both parties have to want to work on it. I'm not matter-of-fact about this, I've struggled with it. But I know it's the right thing for me. I hope we can continue to be friends," I said.

There was a long silence. He took his arm away from my shoulders and stared into my eyes. "I can't do that, Darla. I can't hang out with you and your friends, I can't call you up and have coffee. I care about you deeply, and I don't know how to care about you less. I guess it's all or nothing, and you say it can't be all. Then it will have to be nothing," he countered.

"Well, it won't be nothing, exactly. We'll run into other during the Carstairs case until it's over," I argued.

"I doubt we'll have occasion to run into each other, even in the Carstairs case. You'll be dealing with local law enforcement or agents in charge of the case."

So that was that.

"What now?" I asked. "Do you want to walk a little more, or call it a day?"

"Let's walk a little more, Darla. I have to process this. I'm not ready to just walk away. You've really taken me by surprise," he said.

We walked the gardens for another half hour or so, talking little, and when we did it was only about the gardens not about us. We headed out to the parking lot and I held his hand to pull him to my car.

"I'm really sorry, Paul. I think you're fantastic. I'm sorry to hurt you," I said.

"What's done is done, Darla. I'll miss you, there's no doubt about that. But we're both adults, we've been here before. At least I have. Take care of yourself," he said. He gave me a quick kiss and walked away.

I felt awful. I felt proud. I felt alone. I felt strong. I felt fearful. I had better mean what I said because there was no going back now. I got into the car, rolled down the windows, and stayed there for a long time. Finally, I cranked up the engine and drove out of the parking lot to find a hotel for the night.

Chapter 25

Turned out Allie wasn't as tight-lipped as I thought she'd be. She had been hoping to stay in a situation that would enable her to continue to enjoy the clothes, jewelry, and lifestyle she'd come to appreciate. There was no chance of that, given what she'd done. When I went down to the station on Monday to complete all the red tape and paperwork, Officer Johnson agreed to meet with me afterward.

"I suppose Agent Harbinville has told you that none of the parties charged have chosen to go through a trial. Except Schwindle, of course. That's what started this whole mess."

Her jawline hardened. Paul hadn't told me that, but I didn't let on. She continued, "So I'm able to give you more information than I otherwise might. In fact, all the statements will be public record as soon as they're processed."

"So what can you tell me now?" I prompted.

"Turns out Glenys McCoy, Allie to you, didn't give her accomplice Meurtrier the full story. She and Jackson Mendel, Jake to you, split the money he siphoned off Schwindle's accounts for her. She got a little more than him, but he got a pretty big haul. While she was buying expensive jewelry to flash around, he was keeping a low profile while apparently working with the same jewelers to convert his portion to gemstones. Detective Rodriguez and the FBI are tracking down that angle. We may never know why he chose jewels unless one of the jewelers talks. Maybe he figured it would be easier to transport that way, or harder to trace."

Officer Johnson stopped and smiled. "You should have seen her face when we asked her about the jewels. She was looking for money, didn't know he'd converted it to anything else."

"So how will you recoup the money she spent on designers clothes and jewelry?" I asked.

"Not my department. That'll be up to the District Attorney's office. My guess is they'll confiscate anything of value and fine her for the rest. Probably never see a penny. Oh, and something else you might be interested in." She paused for dramatic effect, as if she hadn't had my full attention the whole time.

"What?" I asked.

"Meurtrier wasn't the one who started your fire. She was." Officer Johnson clearly expected a response she didn't get from me. I stayed silent as the final pieces clicked into place in my brain.

I'd felt all along that Allie was the strongest of the group, that she had a bigger hand in all the events than law enforcement officers had given her credit for. She was the "neighbor" that the others followed. The leader who stepped in and took a personal role when her followers failed.

Officer Johnson cleared her throat.

"Is there more?" I asked.

"That's about it. With Mendel dead and Meurtrier believing all the lies McCoy told him, we'll never know the truth. She's a slippery one. Whether she was ever going to testify, or still will, or whether she was just going to skip the country first chance she got. Whether she was going to let Mendel keep his portion, or kill him out of greed. Whether she was ever going to pay off anyone, or keep all of it herself. Even Schwindle probably doesn't know, or won't say, how much she got away with. The best thing for you, Ms. King, is to realize that this batch of crooks isn't likely to do any more damage to you. Put it behind you and go on."

Put it behind me and go on. Good advice for several parts of my life. I was trying.

I thanked Officer Johnson for talking with me and headed home. As usual, there was lots of information Paul hadn't chosen to share with me, though he would have said I didn't need to know. It was his nature, I couldn't blame him for it. Especially now that we were no longer a couple.

Maybe now I could concentrate on Heather and her engagement party. Or on my complicated love life. Who'd have thought at my age I'd be wrestling with romance?

Chapter 26

The engagement party was going great. When I'd passed on Doug's invitation to host the party out here at his place, I was sure Heather would decline. I was wrong. She and Micah jumped at the chance to have their party out in the country. So I made little maps with directions to the ranch to slip into the invitations. I told them to look for the giant stand of prickly pear cactus at the gate, the one Doug was famous for.

Now Heather and Micah and a couple dozen of their friends were finishing up their meal, laughing, and by all appearances having a great time. Doug was the chef. He'd gotten up in the wee hours this morning to put the ribs and brisket on the big pit in the yard, and he tended it all morning. When we served lunch about an hour ago, the food met with solid approval. I'd stocked coolers with beer, Snapple, and water. Now there were more Snapple and water bottles on the tables than beer bottles. Micah brought his own sound system, with speakers much more powerful than mine. I didn't recognize many of the songs but liked his choice of music anyway.

Even the weather cooperated. Although the sun was out, the temperature hadn't yet gotten out of the 80s. That was lucky in late May, when we never knew if we'd face heat, cold, or rain. Heather looked very much the confident hostess as she visited with friends. When I looked at her I still saw the toddler she had been, and I was trying hard to look beyond the child to see the capable young woman she had become.

On the veranda, Doug walked up behind me and wrapped his arms around my waist. We stood like that for a while, watching Heather and Micah and their friends out in the yard, not saying a word. I leaned my head back against his shoulder and he put his lips against my ear.

"It's a beautiful thing, isn't it?" he asked.

"What?"

"Commitment," he said.

I'm sure he felt me stiffen in his arms, because he chuckled and held me closer.

"Don't worry, Darla. I'm not pressuring you. Just letting you know that when you're ready to talk about it, we can. I'm a patient man."

"You've got to admit, I've come a long way," I said.

I twisted around in the circle of his arms until we faced each other. I walked him backward around the corner of the house out of view. I kissed him and said, "Time is speeding by faster and faster these days, Doug. I might just be ready sooner than you think."

With his arms still encircling my waist he spun us both around, flattened me against the wall of the house, and kissed me back.